DRAGONS
RIDERS OF BERK

VOLUME SIX

UNDERWORLD

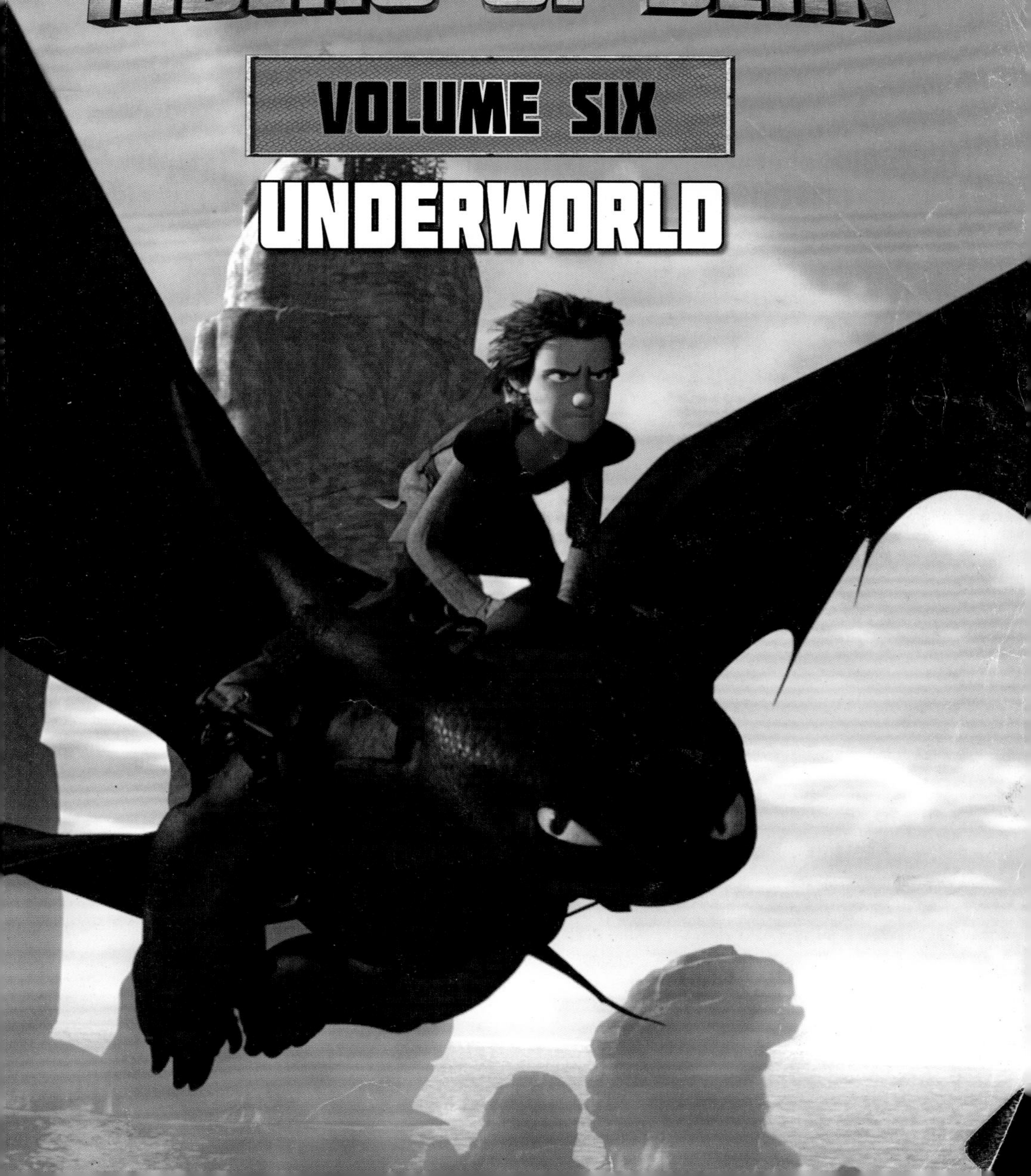

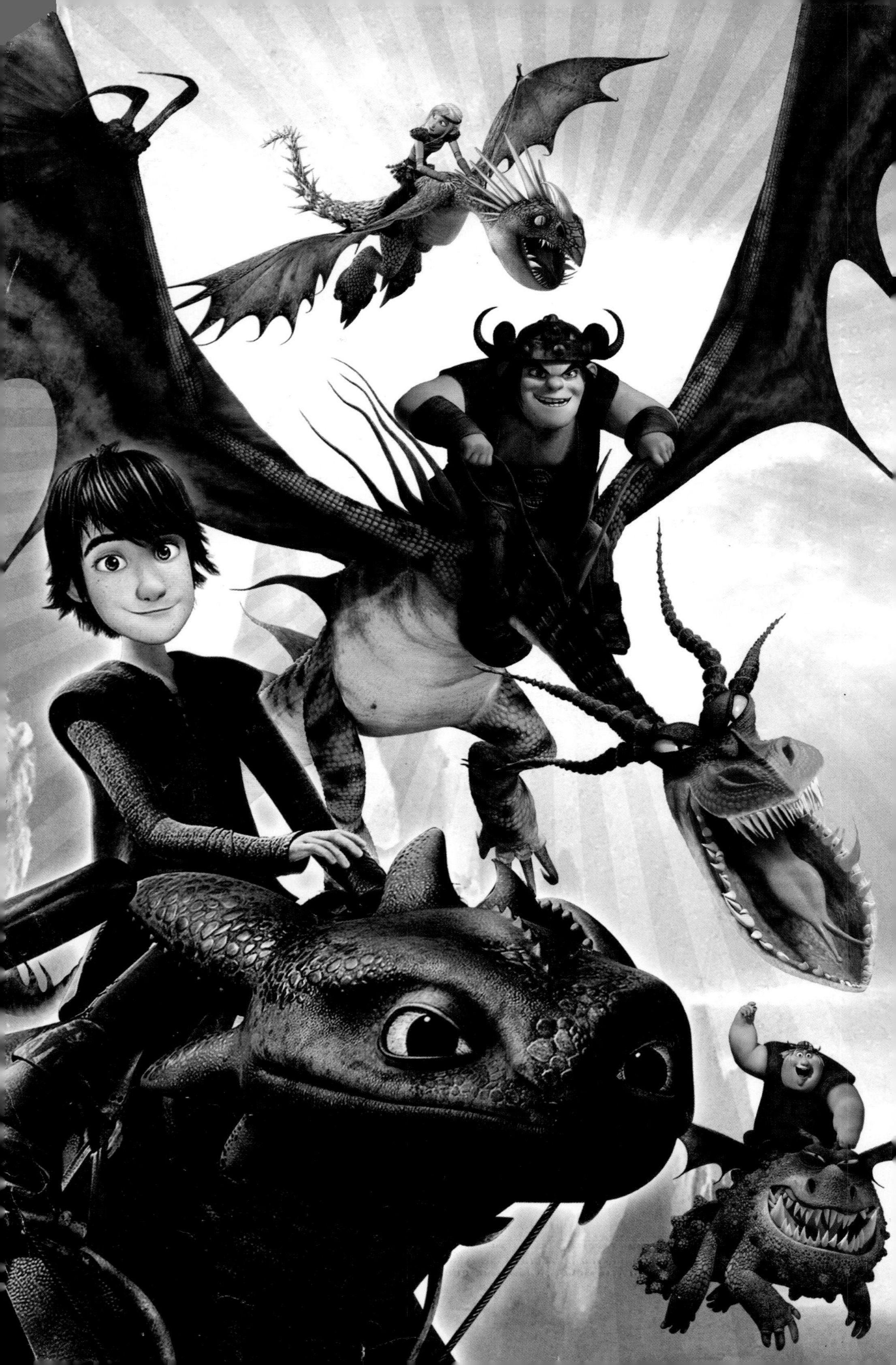

DREAMWORKS DRAGONS RIDERS OF BERK

VOLUME SIX

UNDERWORLD

SCRIPT
SIMON FURMAN

ART
IWAN NAZIF

COLORING
DIGIKORE

LETTERING
JIM CAMPBELL

TITAN
COMICS

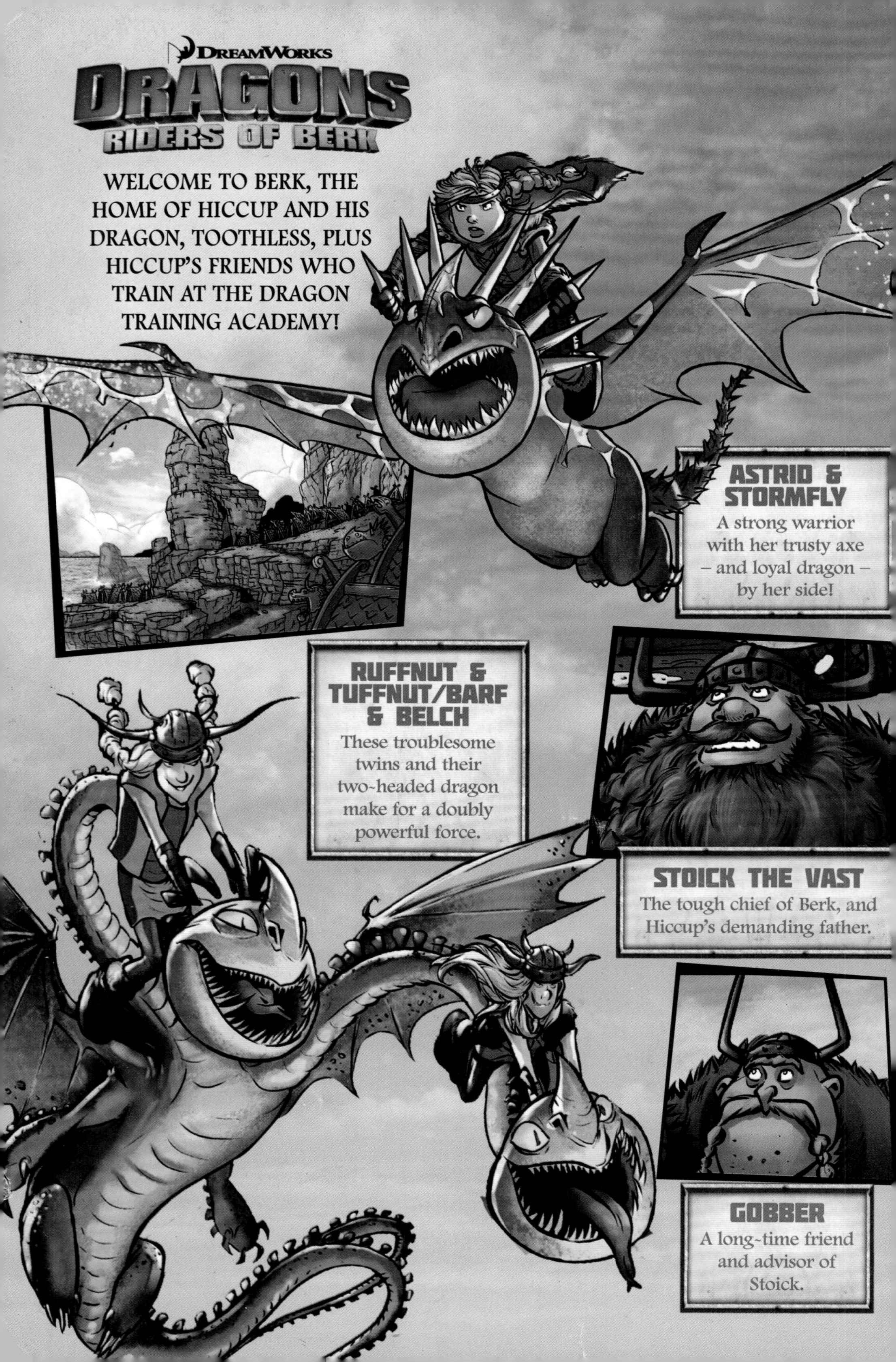
DREAMWORKS
DRAGONS
RIDERS OF BERK
WELCOME TO BERK, THE HOME OF HICCUP AND HIS DRAGON, TOOTHLESS, PLUS HICCUP'S FRIENDS WHO TRAIN AT THE DRAGON TRAINING ACADEMY!
ASTRID & STORMFLY
A strong warrior with her trusty axe – and loyal dragon – by her side!
RUFFNUT & TUFFNUT/BARF & BELCH
These troublesome twins and their two-headed dragon make for a doubly powerful force.
STOICK THE VAST
The tough chief of Berk, and Hiccup's demanding father.
GOBBER
A long-time friend and advisor of Stoick.

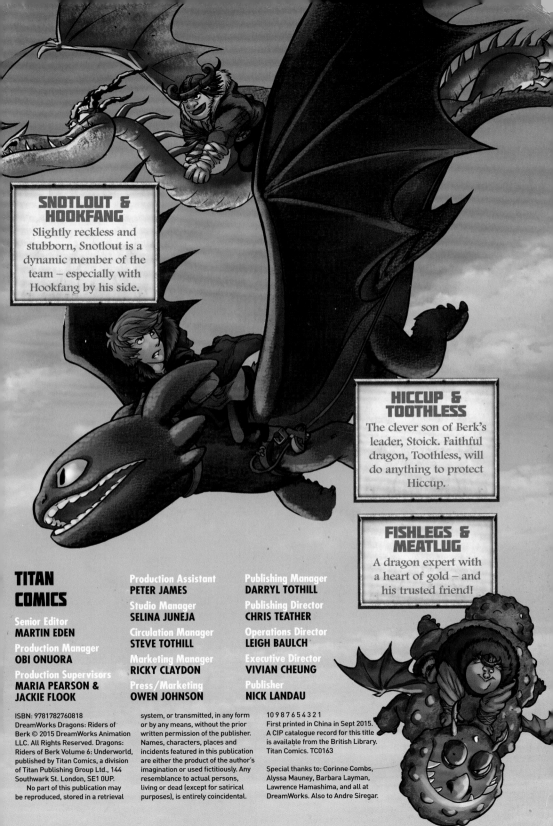

SNOTLOUT & HOOKFANG

Slightly reckless and stubborn, Snotlout is a dynamic member of the team – especially with Hookfang by his side.

HICCUP & TOOTHLESS

The clever son of Berk's leader, Stoick. Faithful dragon, Toothless, will do anything to protect Hiccup.

FISHLEGS & MEATLUG

A dragon expert with a heart of gold – and his trusted friend!

TITAN COMICS

Senior Editor
MARTIN EDEN

Production Manager
OBI ONUORA

Production Supervisors
MARIA PEARSON &
JACKIE FLOOK

Production Assistant
PETER JAMES

Studio Manager
SELINA JUNEJA

Circulation Manager
STEVE TOTHILL

Marketing Manager
RICKY CLAYDON

Press/Marketing
OWEN JOHNSON

Publishing Manager
DARRYL TOTHILL

Publishing Director
CHRIS TEATHER

Operations Director
LEIGH BAULCH

Executive Director
VIVIAN CHEUNG

Publisher
NICK LANDAU

ISBN: 9781782760818
DreamWorks Dragons: Riders of Berk © 2015 DreamWorks Animation LLC. All Rights Reserved. Dragons: Riders of Berk Volume 6: Underworld, published by Titan Comics, a division of Titan Publishing Group Ltd., 144 Southwark St. London, SE1 0UP.

No part of this publication may be reproduced, stored in a retrieval system, or transmitted, in any form or by any means, without the prior written permission of the publisher. Names, characters, places and incidents featured in this publication are either the product of the author's imagination or used fictitiously. Any resemblance to actual persons, living or dead (except for satirical purposes), is entirely coincidental.

10 9 8 7 6 5 4 3 2 1
First printed in China in Sept 2015. A CIP catalogue record for this title is available from the British Library. Titan Comics. TC0163

Special thanks to: Corinne Combs, Alyssa Mauney, Barbara Layman, Lawrence Hamashima, and all at DreamWorks. Also to Andre Siregar.

CHAPTER ONE

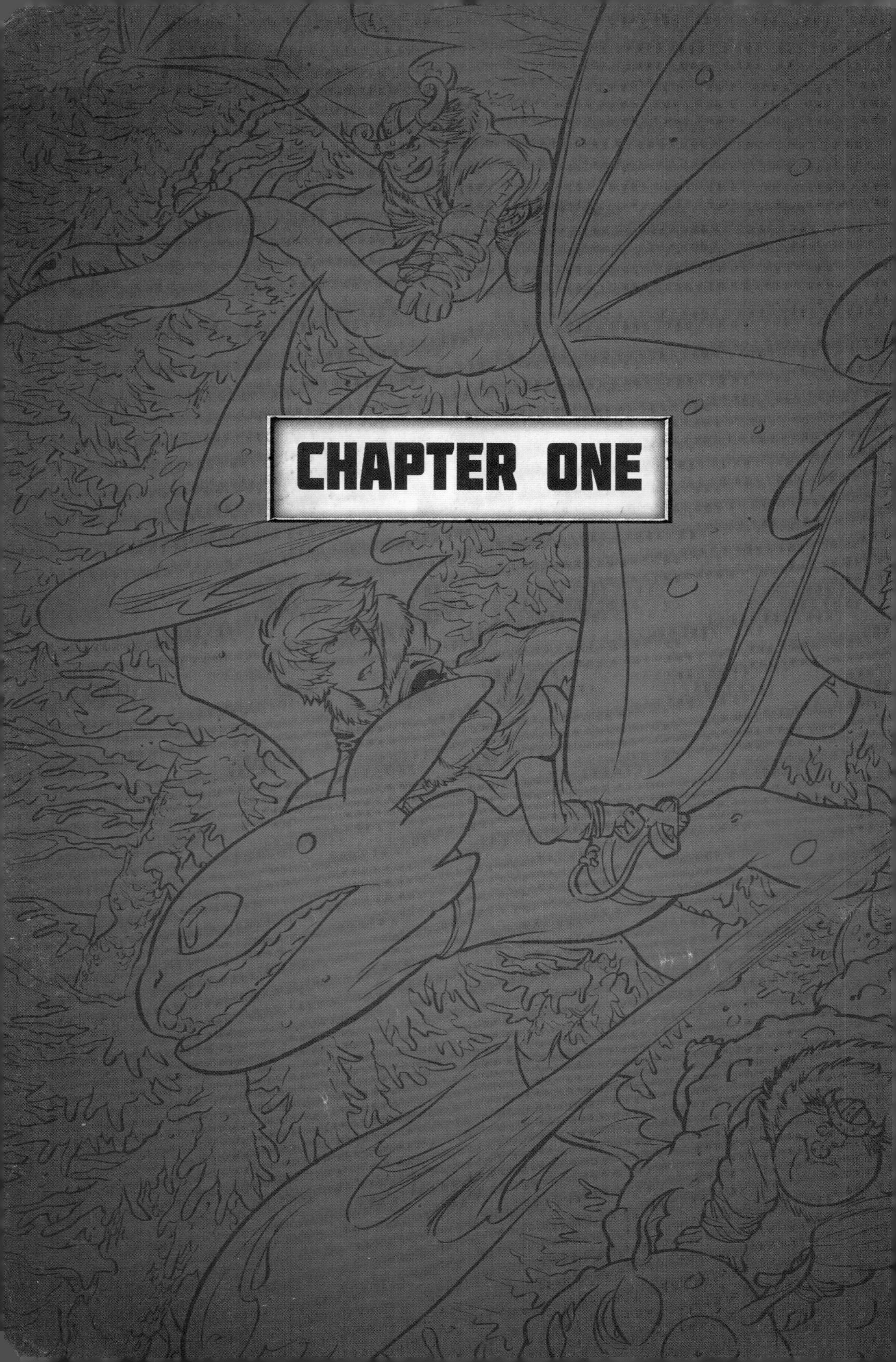

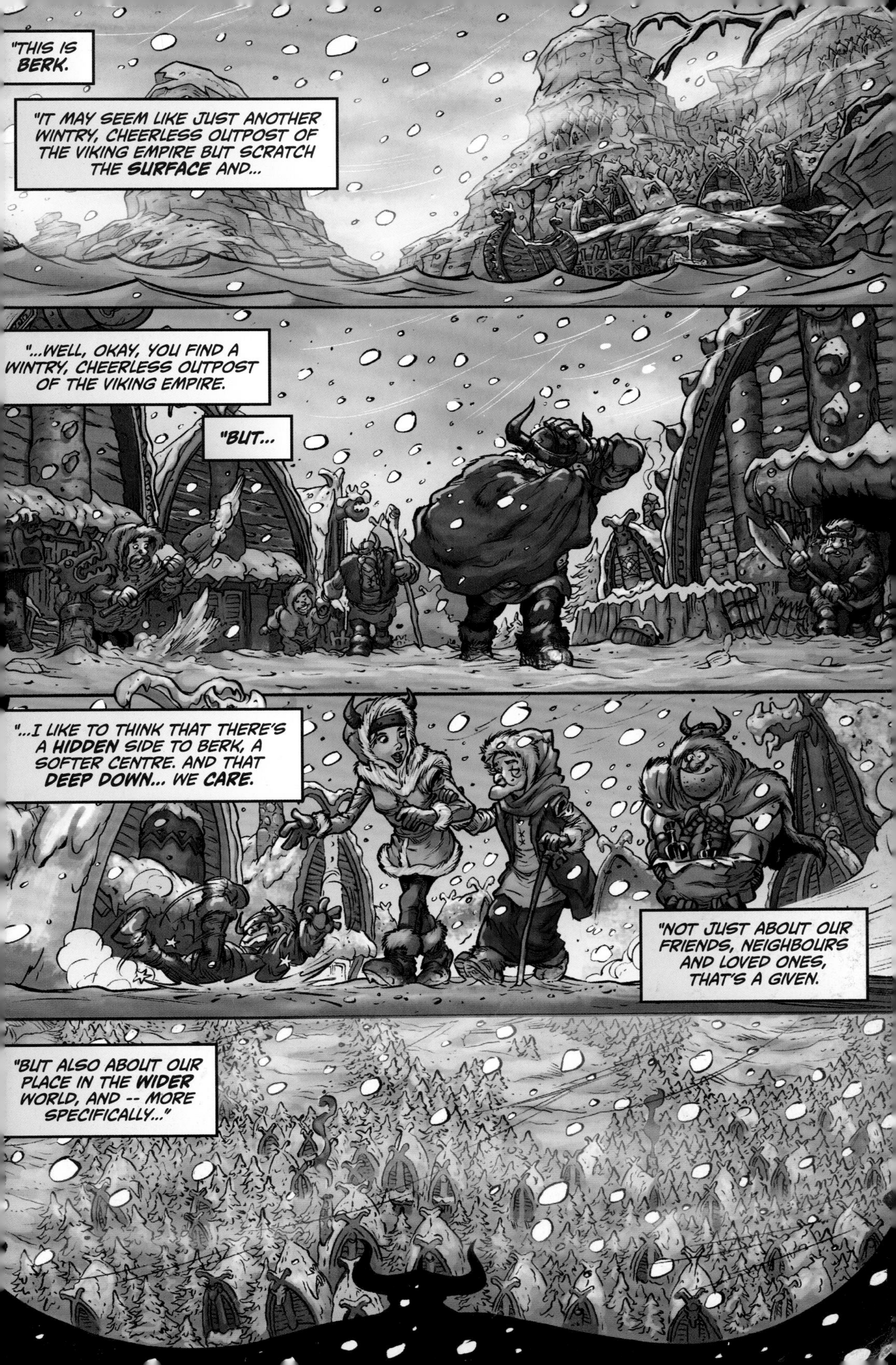
"THIS IS BERK.
"IT MAY SEEM LIKE JUST ANOTHER WINTRY, CHEERLESS OUTPOST OF THE VIKING EMPIRE BUT SCRATCH THE SURFACE AND...
"...WELL, OKAY, YOU FIND A WINTRY, CHEERLESS OUTPOST OF THE VIKING EMPIRE.
"BUT...
"...I LIKE TO THINK THAT THERE'S A HIDDEN SIDE TO BERK, A SOFTER CENTRE. AND THAT DEEP DOWN... WE CARE.
"NOT JUST ABOUT OUR FRIENDS, NEIGHBOURS AND LOVED ONES, THAT'S A GIVEN.
"BUT ALSO ABOUT OUR PLACE IN THE WIDER WORLD, AND -- MORE SPECIFICALLY..."

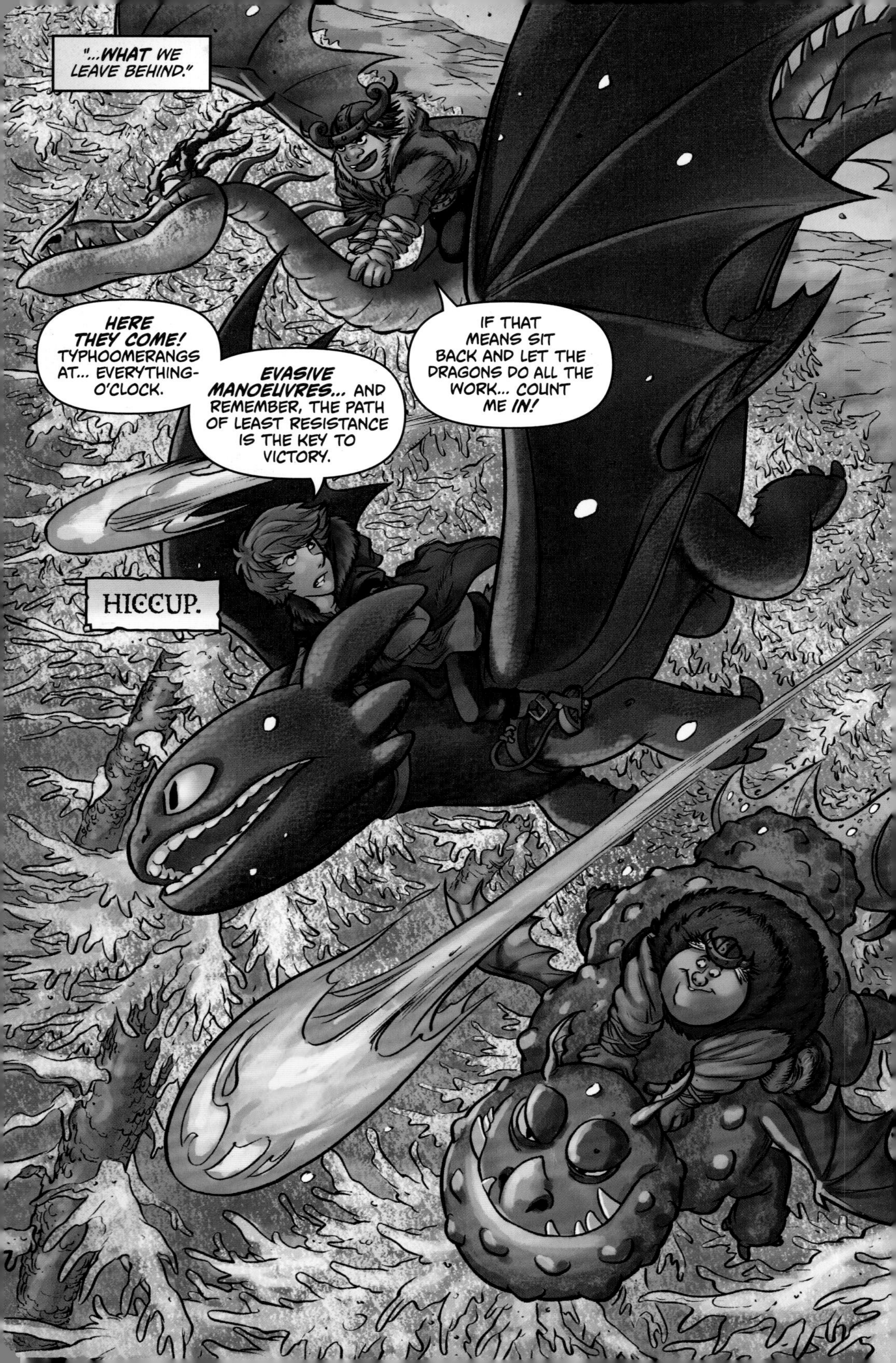
"...WHAT WE LEAVE BEHIND."
HERE THEY COME! TYPHOOMERANGS AT... EVERYTHING-O'CLOCK.
EVASIVE MANOEUVRES... AND REMEMBER, THE PATH OF LEAST RESISTANCE IS THE KEY TO VICTORY.
IF THAT MEANS SIT BACK AND LET THE DRAGONS DO ALL THE WORK... COUNT ME IN!
HICCUP.

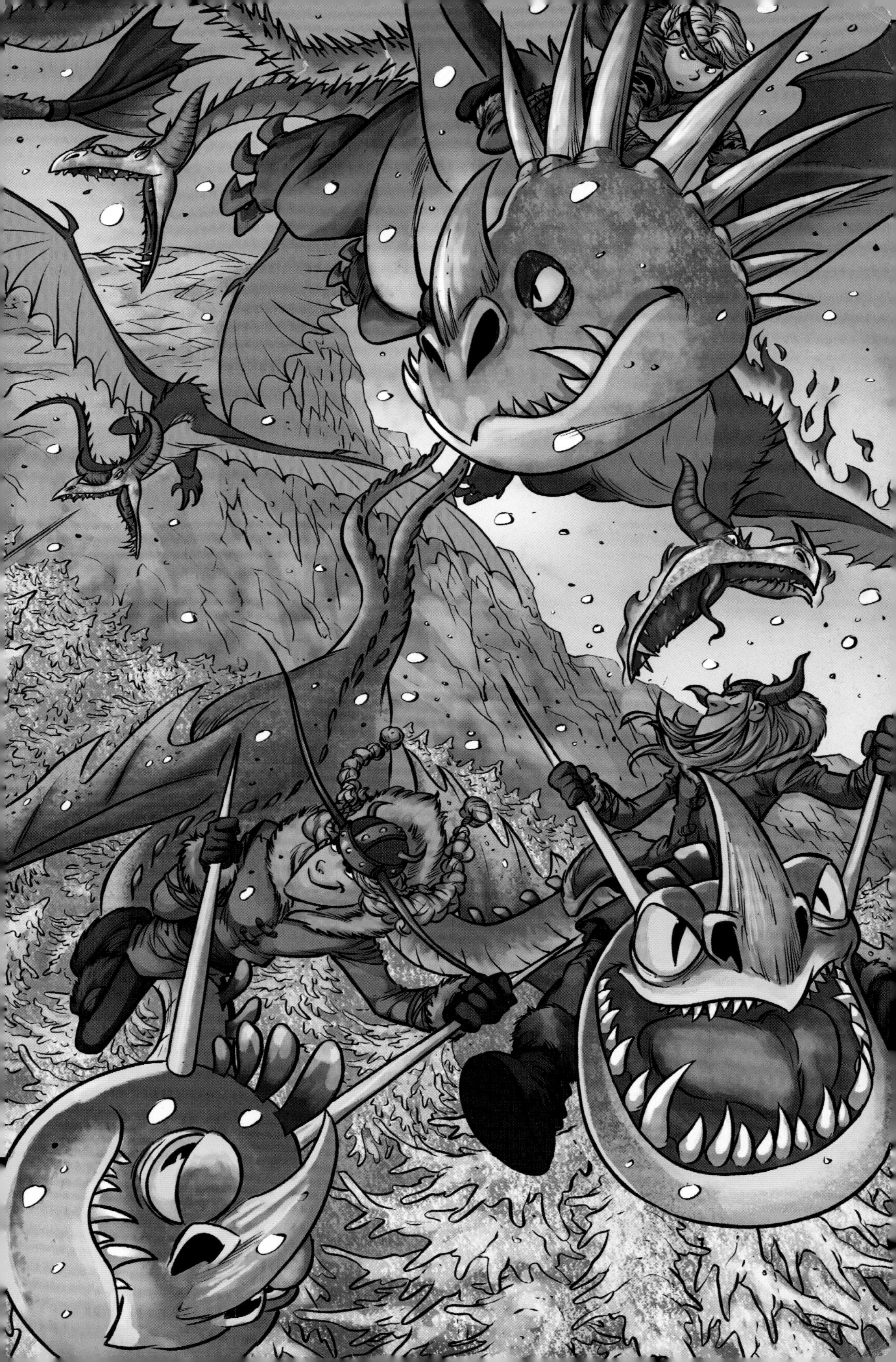

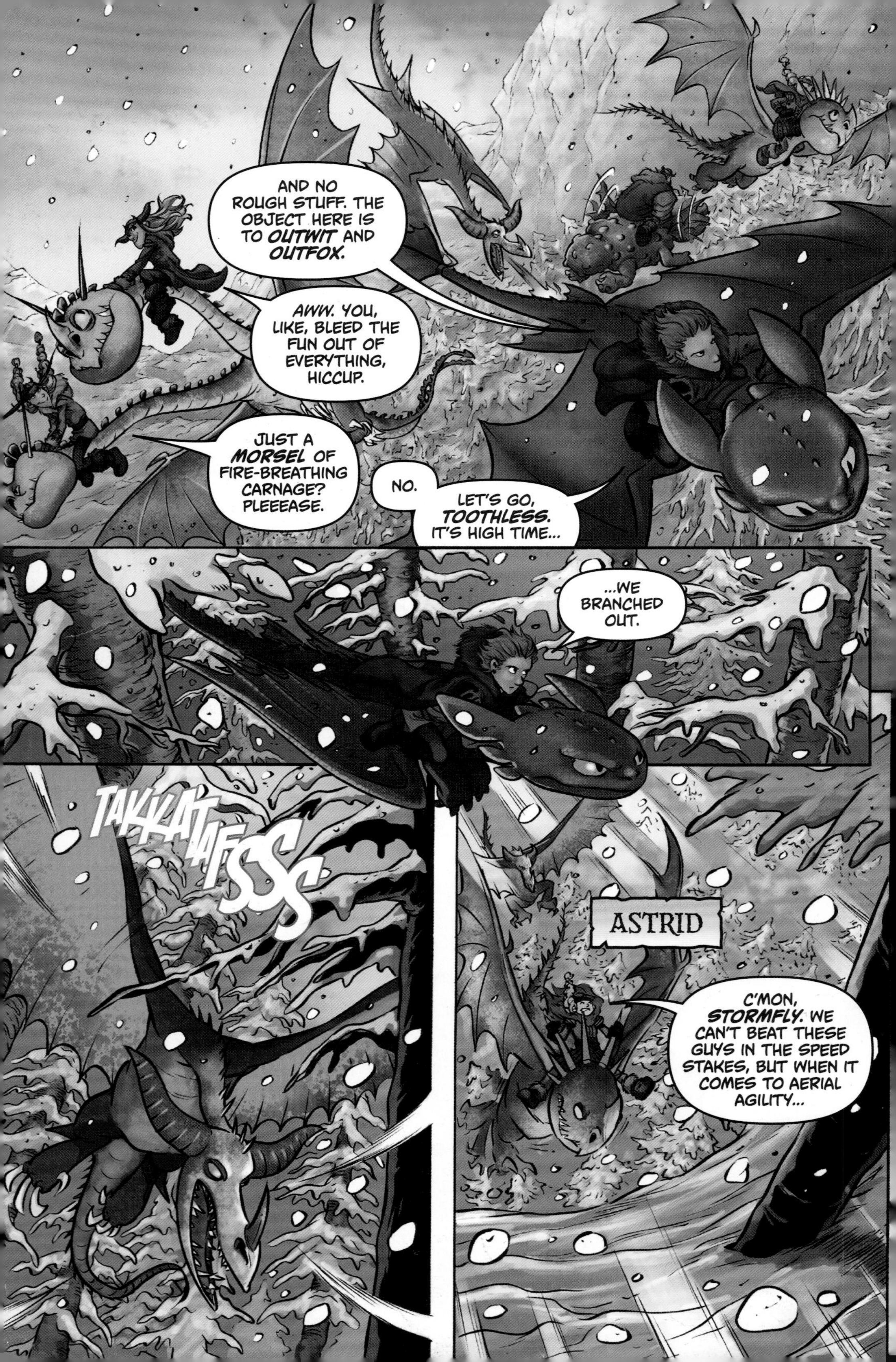
AND NO ROUGH STUFF. THE OBJECT HERE IS TO OUTWIT AND OUTFOX.
AWW. YOU, LIKE, BLEED THE FUN OUT OF EVERYTHING, HICCUP.
JUST A MORSEL OF FIRE-BREATHING CARNAGE? PLEEEASE.
NO.
LET'S GO, TOOTHLESS. IT'S HIGH TIME...
...WE BRANCHED OUT.
TAKKATAAFSSS
ASTRID
C'MON, STORMFLY. WE CAN'T BEAT THESE GUYS IN THE SPEED STAKES, BUT WHEN IT COMES TO AERIAL AGILITY...

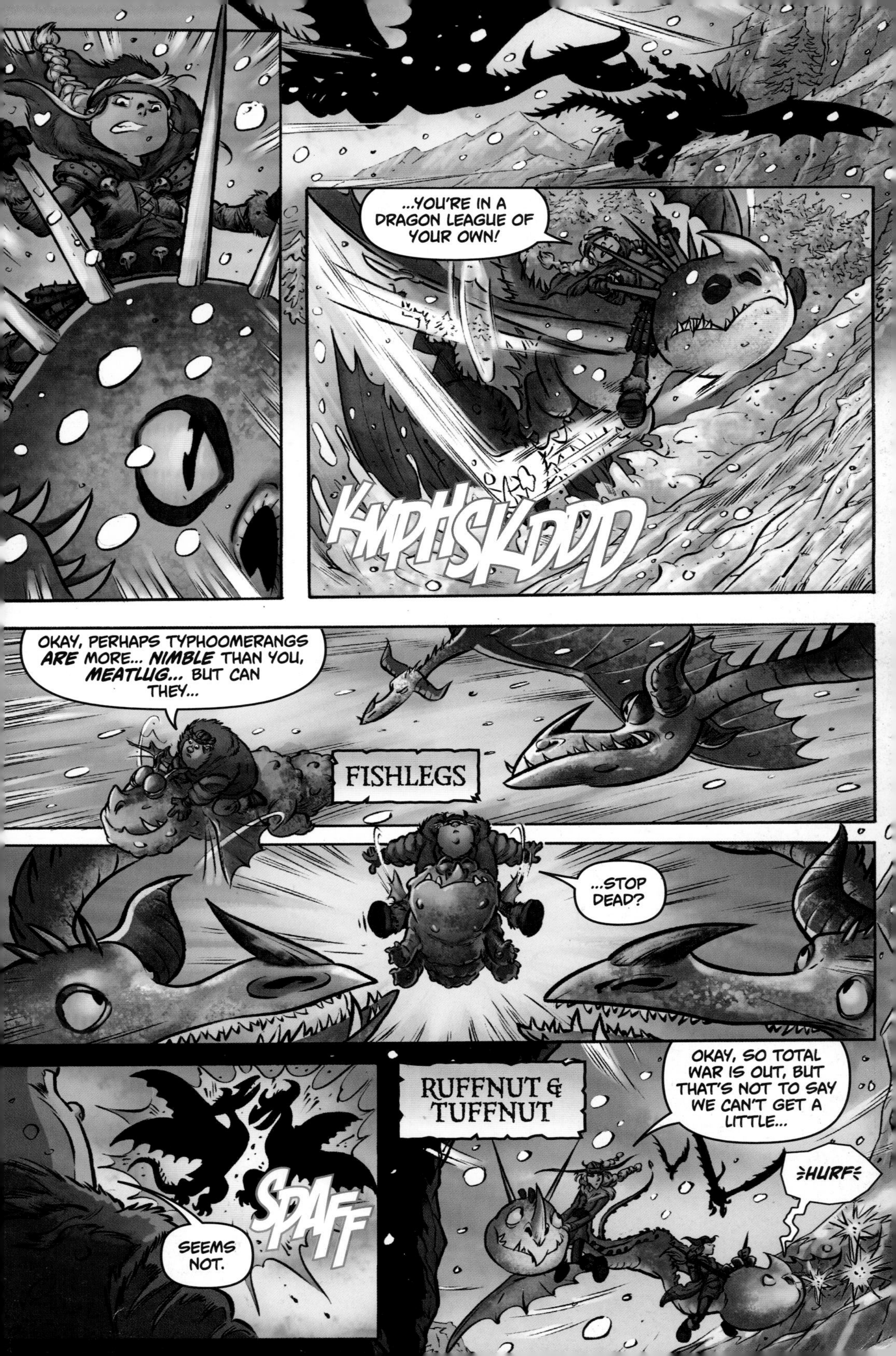

...YOU'RE IN A DRAGON LEAGUE OF YOUR OWN!
KMPHSKDDD
OKAY, PERHAPS TYPHOOMERANGS ARE MORE... NIMBLE THAN YOU, MEATLUG... BUT CAN THEY...
FISHLEGS
...STOP DEAD?
SPAFF
SEEMS NOT.
RUFFNUT & TUFFNUT
OKAY, SO TOTAL WAR IS OUT, BUT THAT'S NOT TO SAY WE CAN'T GET A LITTLE...
HURF

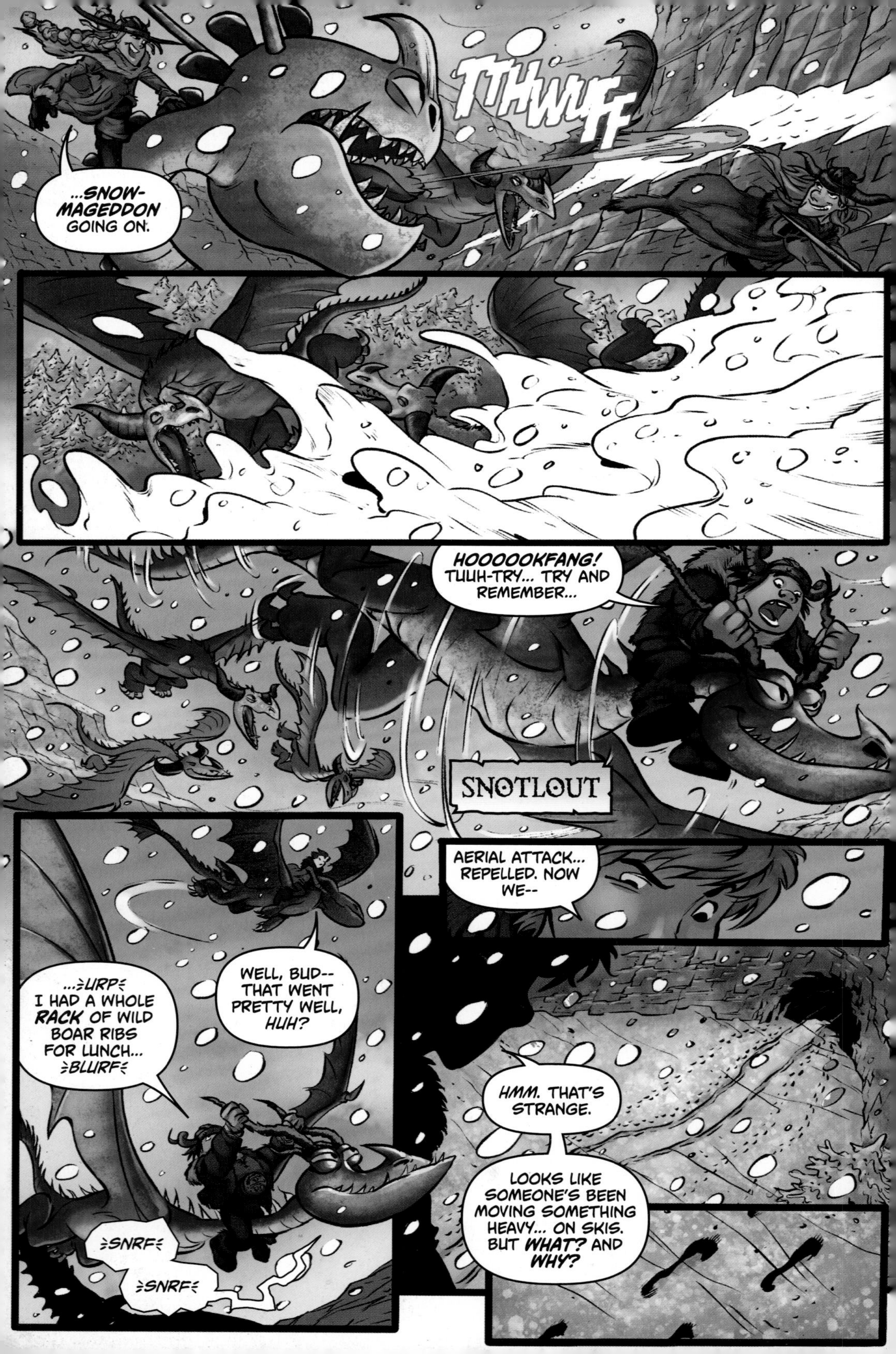

...SNOW-MAGEDDON GOING ON.
TTHWUFF
HOOOOOKFANG! TUUH-TRY... TRY AND REMEMBER...
SNOTLOUT
AERIAL ATTACK... REPELLED. NOW WE--
WELL, BUD-- THAT WENT PRETTY WELL, HUH?
...URP I HAD A WHOLE RACK OF WILD BOAR RIBS FOR LUNCH... BLURF
SNRF
SNRF
HMM. THAT'S STRANGE.
LOOKS LIKE SOMEONE'S BEEN MOVING SOMETHING HEAVY... ON SKIS. BUT WHAT? AND WHY?

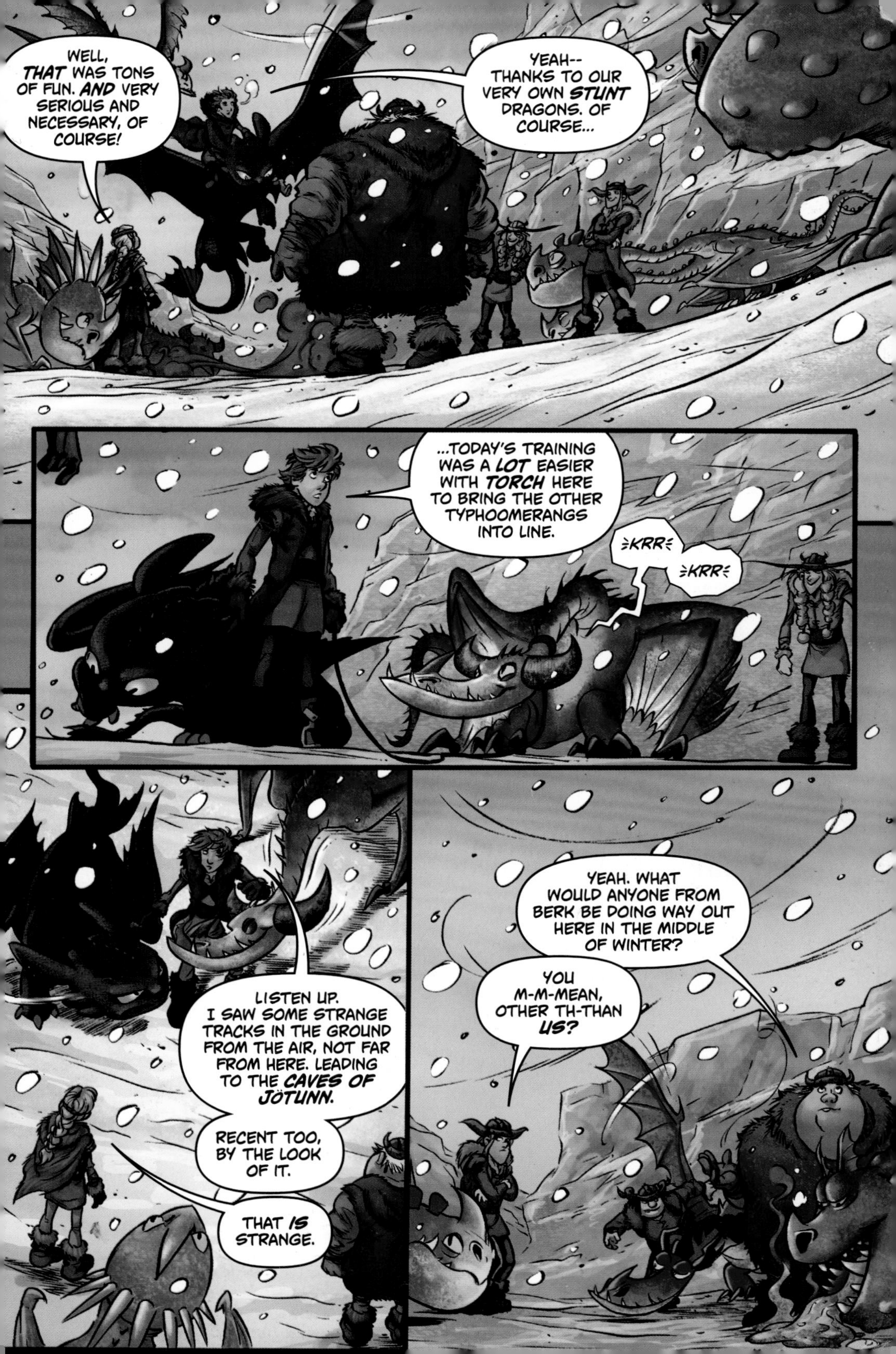
WELL, THAT WAS TONS OF FUN. AND VERY SERIOUS AND NECESSARY, OF COURSE!
YEAH-- THANKS TO OUR VERY OWN STUNT DRAGONS. OF COURSE...
...TODAY'S TRAINING WAS A LOT EASIER WITH TORCH HERE TO BRING THE OTHER TYPHOOMERANGS INTO LINE.
KRR
KRR
LISTEN UP. I SAW SOME STRANGE TRACKS IN THE GROUND FROM THE AIR, NOT FAR FROM HERE. LEADING TO THE CAVES OF JÖTUNN.
RECENT TOO, BY THE LOOK OF IT.
THAT IS STRANGE.
YEAH. WHAT WOULD ANYONE FROM BERK BE DOING WAY OUT HERE IN THE MIDDLE OF WINTER?
YOU M-M-MEAN, OTHER TH-THAN US?

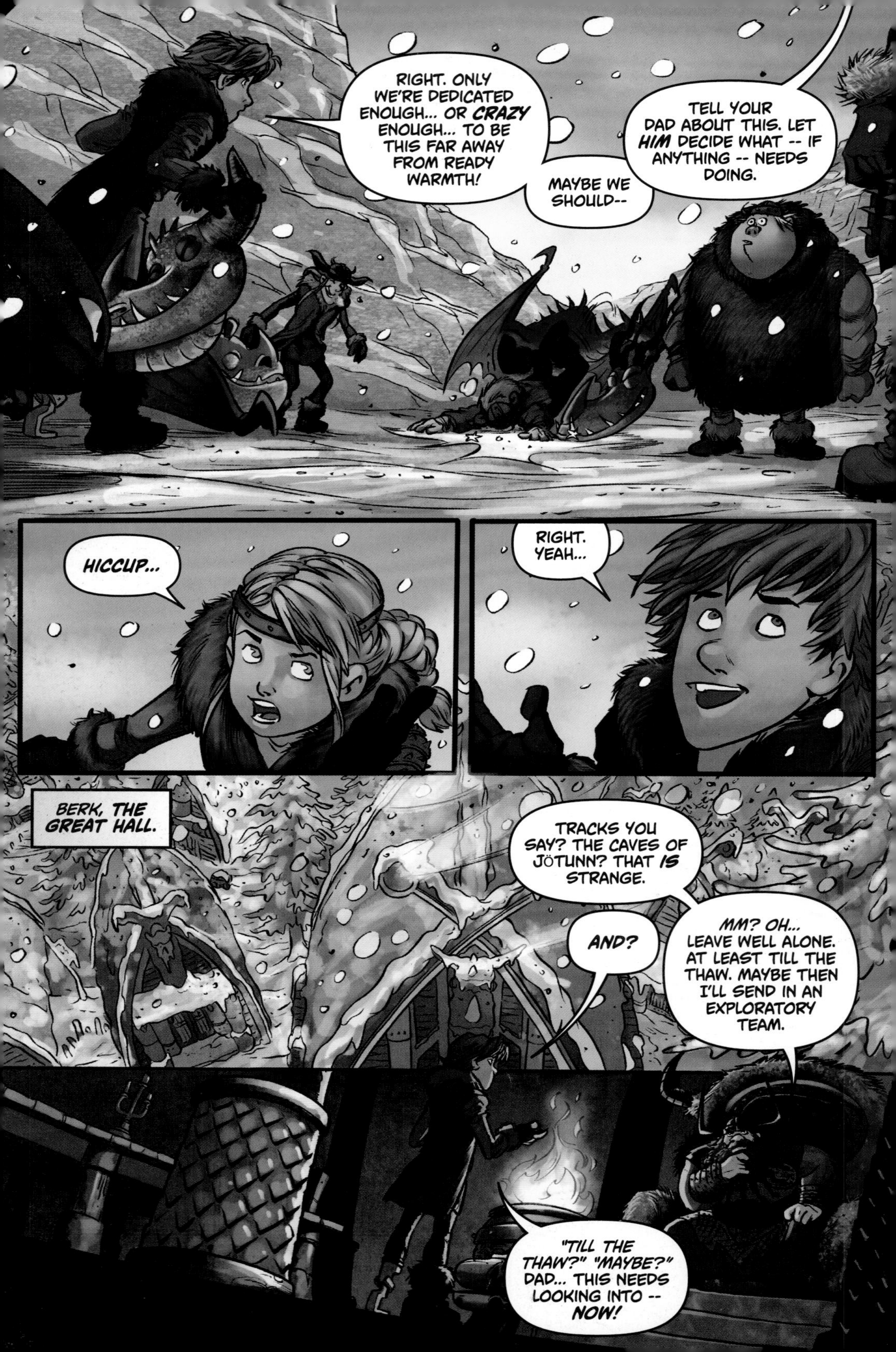
RIGHT. ONLY WE'RE DEDICATED ENOUGH... OR CRAZY ENOUGH... TO BE THIS FAR AWAY FROM READY WARMTH!
MAYBE WE SHOULD--
TELL YOUR DAD ABOUT THIS. LET HIM DECIDE WHAT -- IF ANYTHING -- NEEDS DOING.
HICCUP...
RIGHT. YEAH...
BERK, THE GREAT HALL.
TRACKS YOU SAY? THE CAVES OF JÖTUNN? THAT IS STRANGE.
AND?
MM? OH... LEAVE WELL ALONE. AT LEAST TILL THE THAW. MAYBE THEN I'LL SEND IN AN EXPLORATORY TEAM.
"TILL THE THAW?" "MAYBE?" DAD... THIS NEEDS LOOKING INTO -- NOW!

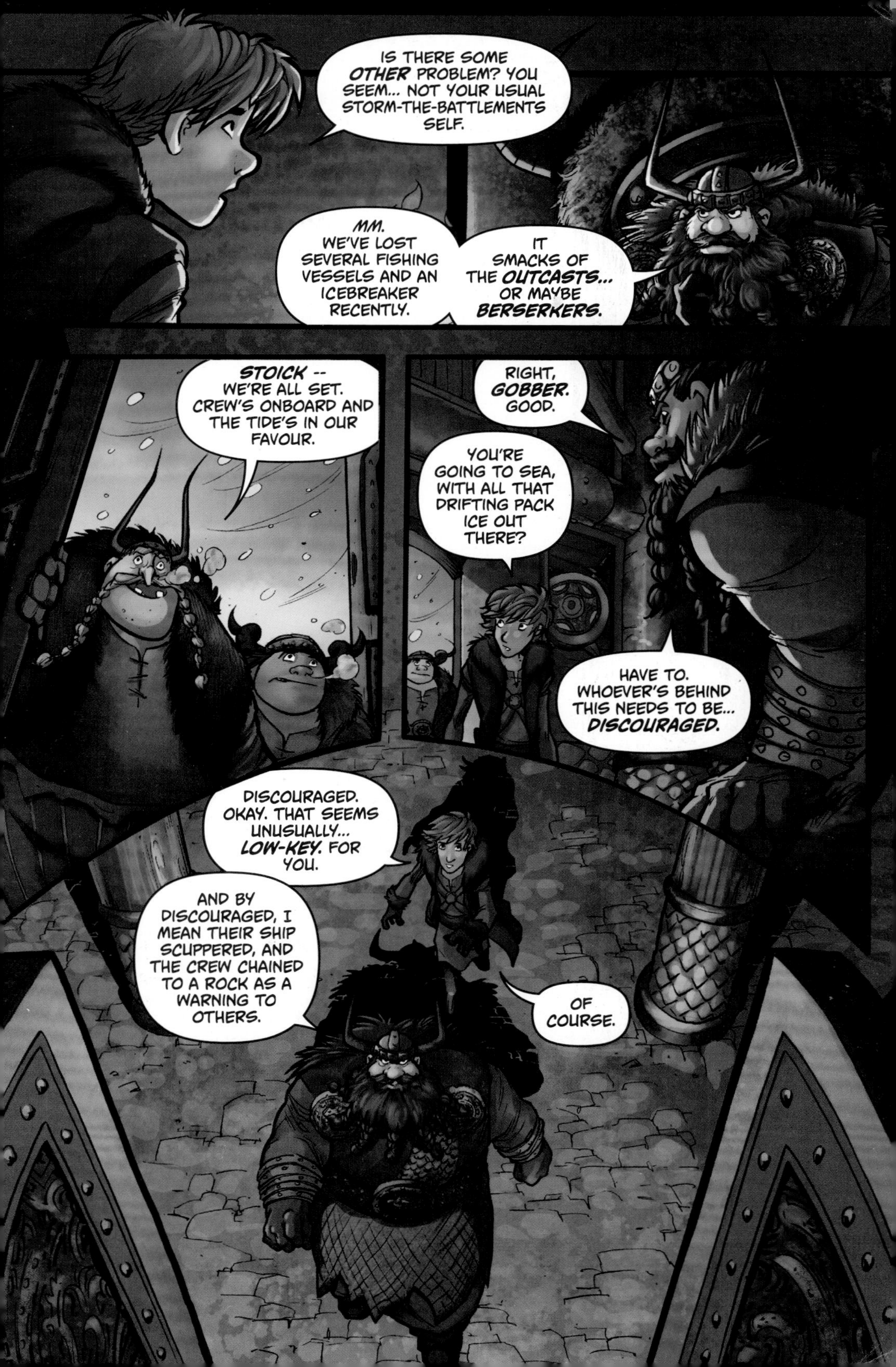
IS THERE SOME OTHER PROBLEM? YOU SEEM... NOT YOUR USUAL STORM-THE-BATTLEMENTS SELF.
MM. WE'VE LOST SEVERAL FISHING VESSELS AND AN ICEBREAKER RECENTLY.
IT SMACKS OF THE OUTCASTS... OR MAYBE BERSERKERS.
STOICK -- WE'RE ALL SET. CREW'S ONBOARD AND THE TIDE'S IN OUR FAVOUR.
RIGHT, GOBBER. GOOD.
YOU'RE GOING TO SEA, WITH ALL THAT DRIFTING PACK ICE OUT THERE?
HAVE TO. WHOEVER'S BEHIND THIS NEEDS TO BE... DISCOURAGED.
DISCOURAGED. OKAY. THAT SEEMS UNUSUALLY... LOW-KEY. FOR YOU.
AND BY DISCOURAGED, I MEAN THEIR SHIP SCUPPERED, AND THE CREW CHAINED TO A ROCK AS A WARNING TO OTHERS.
OF COURSE.

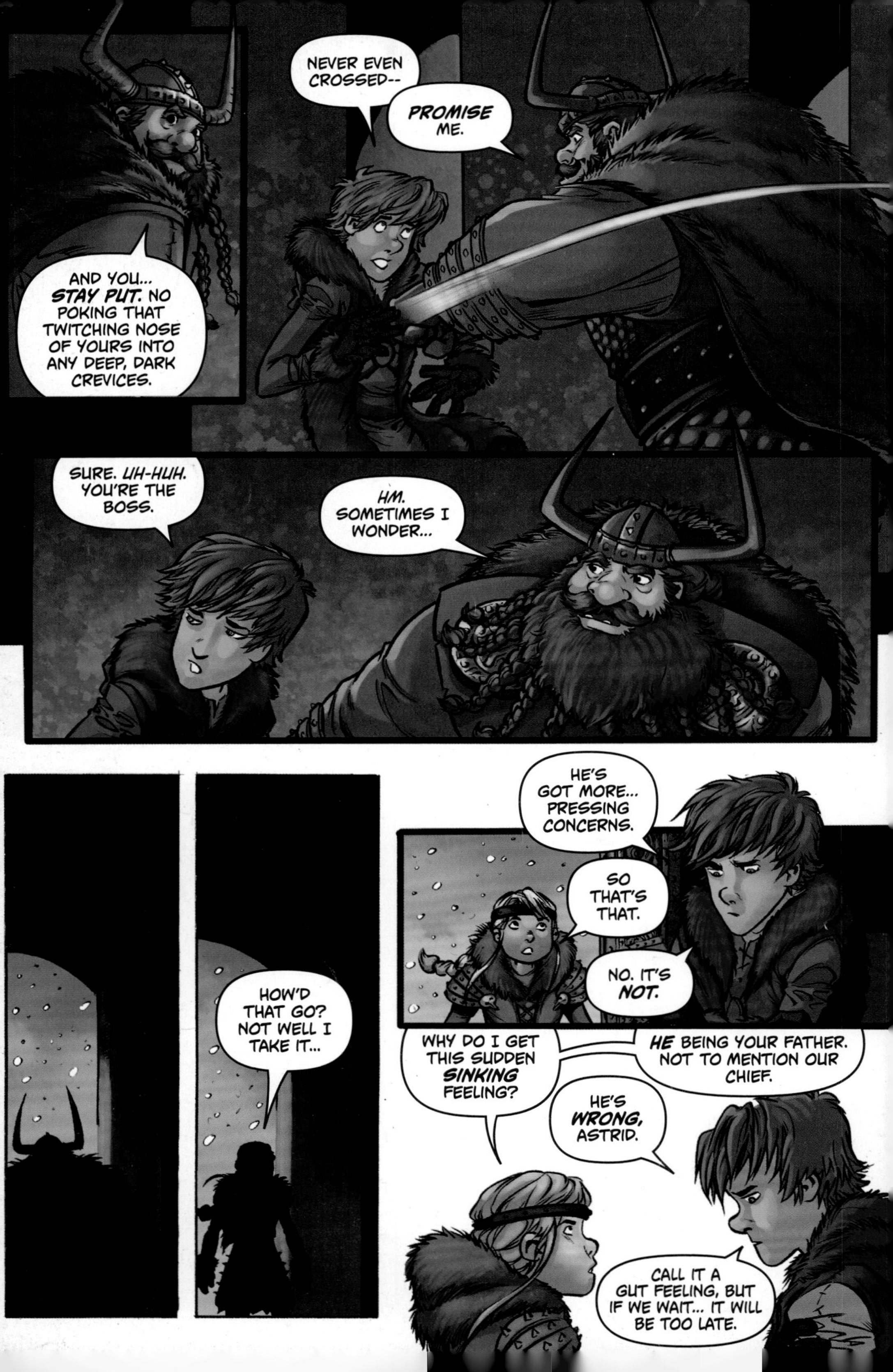
NEVER EVEN CROSSED--
PROMISE ME.
AND YOU... STAY PUT. NO POKING THAT TWITCHING NOSE OF YOURS INTO ANY DEEP, DARK CREVICES.
SURE. UH-HUH. YOU'RE THE BOSS.
HM. SOMETIMES I WONDER...
HOW'D THAT GO? NOT WELL I TAKE IT...
HE'S GOT MORE... PRESSING CONCERNS.
SO THAT'S THAT.
NO. IT'S NOT.
WHY DO I GET THIS SUDDEN SINKING FEELING?
HE BEING YOUR FATHER. NOT TO MENTION OUR CHIEF.
HE'S WRONG, ASTRID.
CALL IT A GUT FEELING, BUT IF WE WAIT... IT WILL BE TOO LATE.

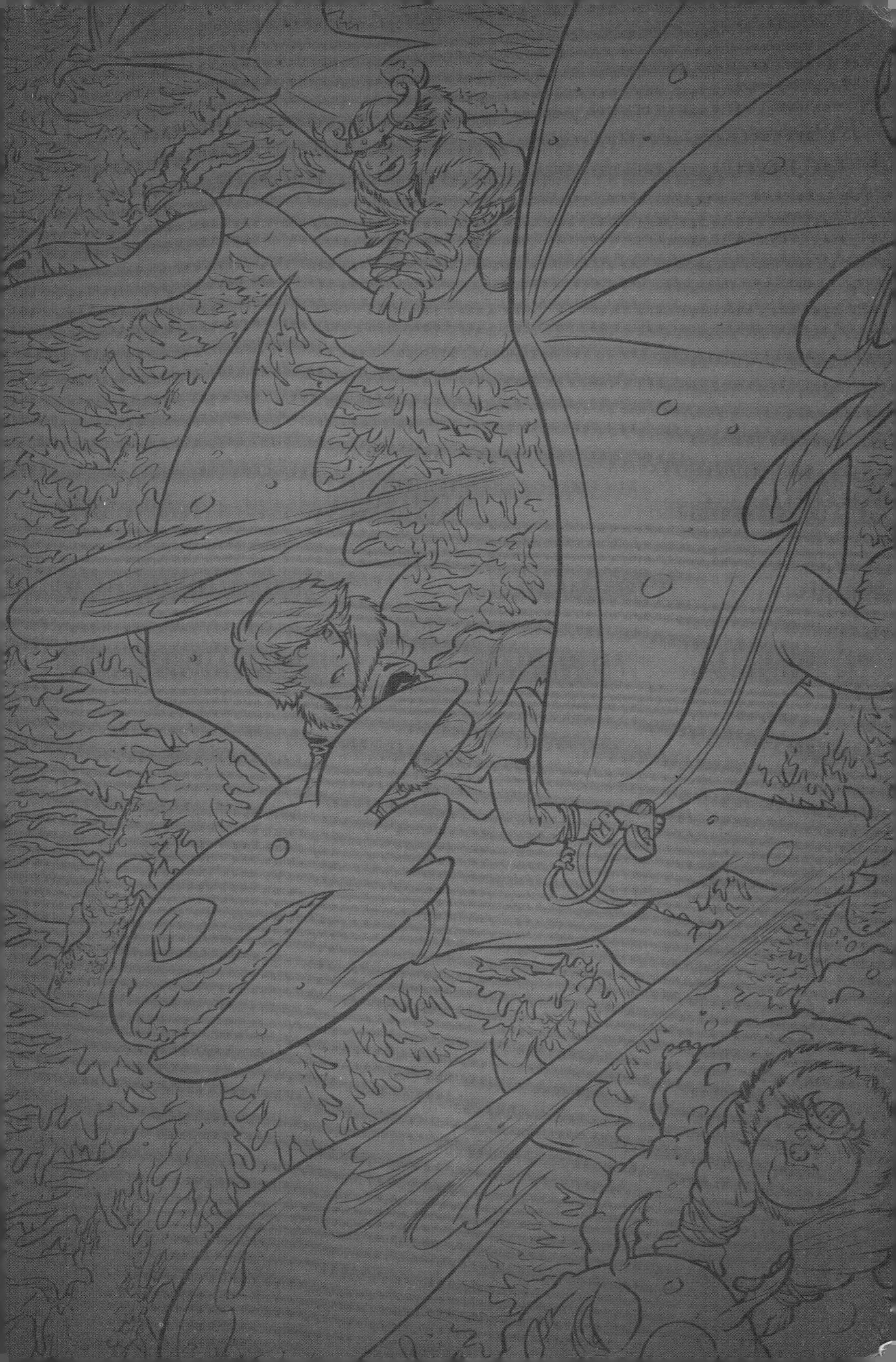

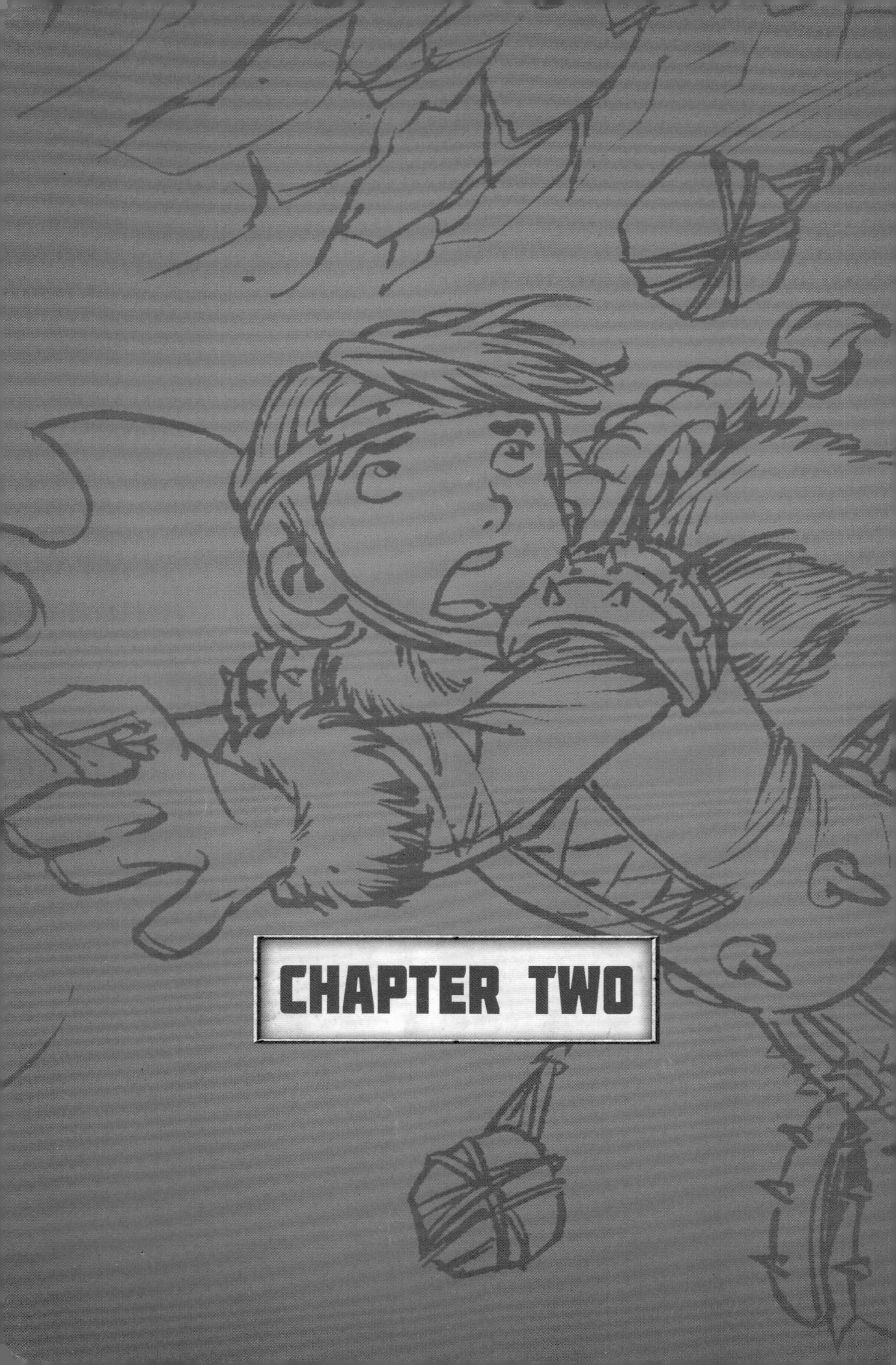

CHAPTER TWO

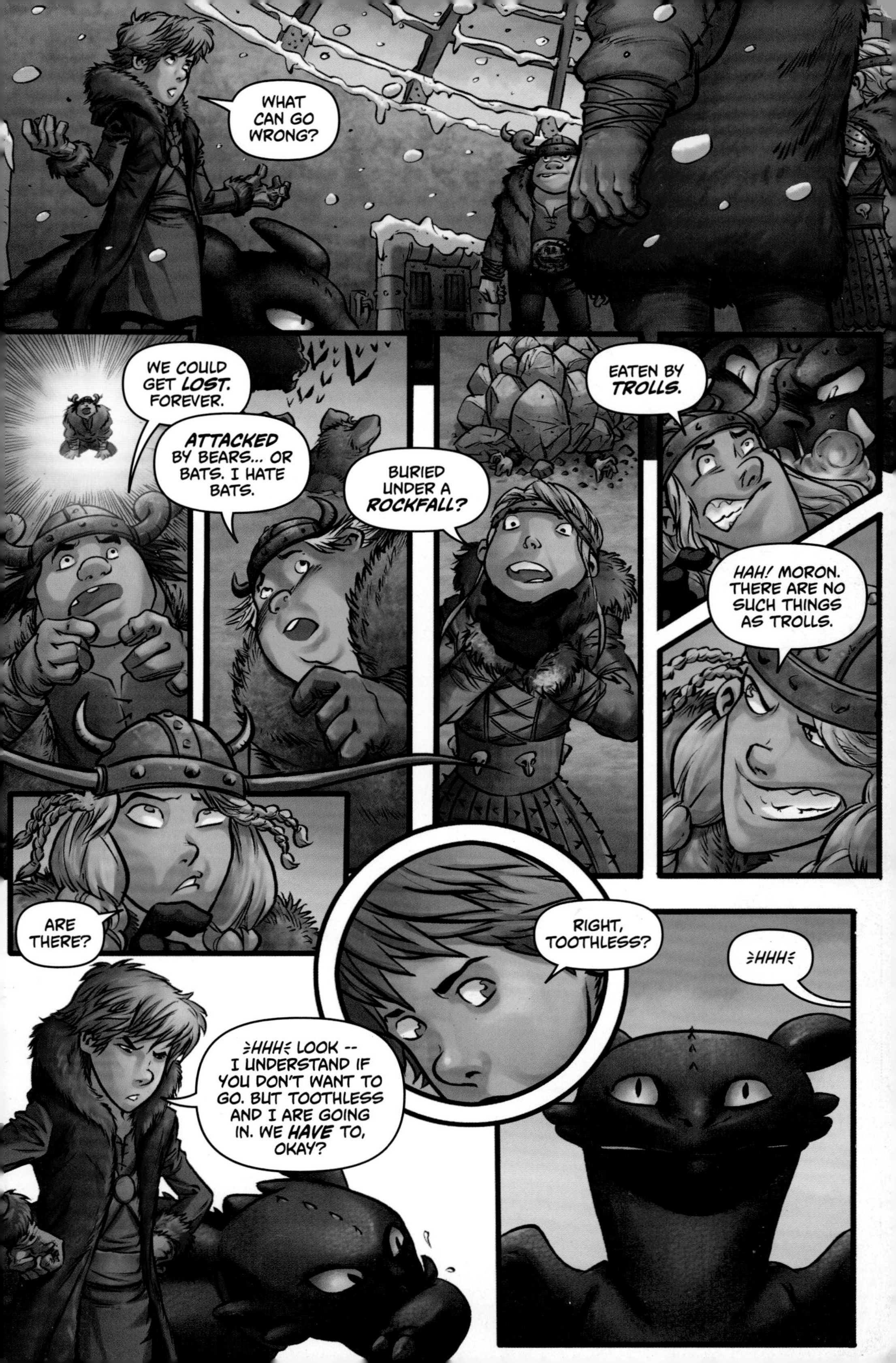
WHAT CAN GO WRONG?
WE COULD GET LOST. FOREVER.
ATTACKED BY BEARS... OR BATS. I HATE BATS.
BURIED UNDER A ROCKFALL?
EATEN BY TROLLS.
HAH! MORON. THERE ARE NO SUCH THINGS AS TROLLS.
ARE THERE?
RIGHT, TOOTHLESS?
HHH
HHH LOOK -- I UNDERSTAND IF YOU DON'T WANT TO GO. BUT TOOTHLESS AND I ARE GOING IN. WE HAVE TO, OKAY?

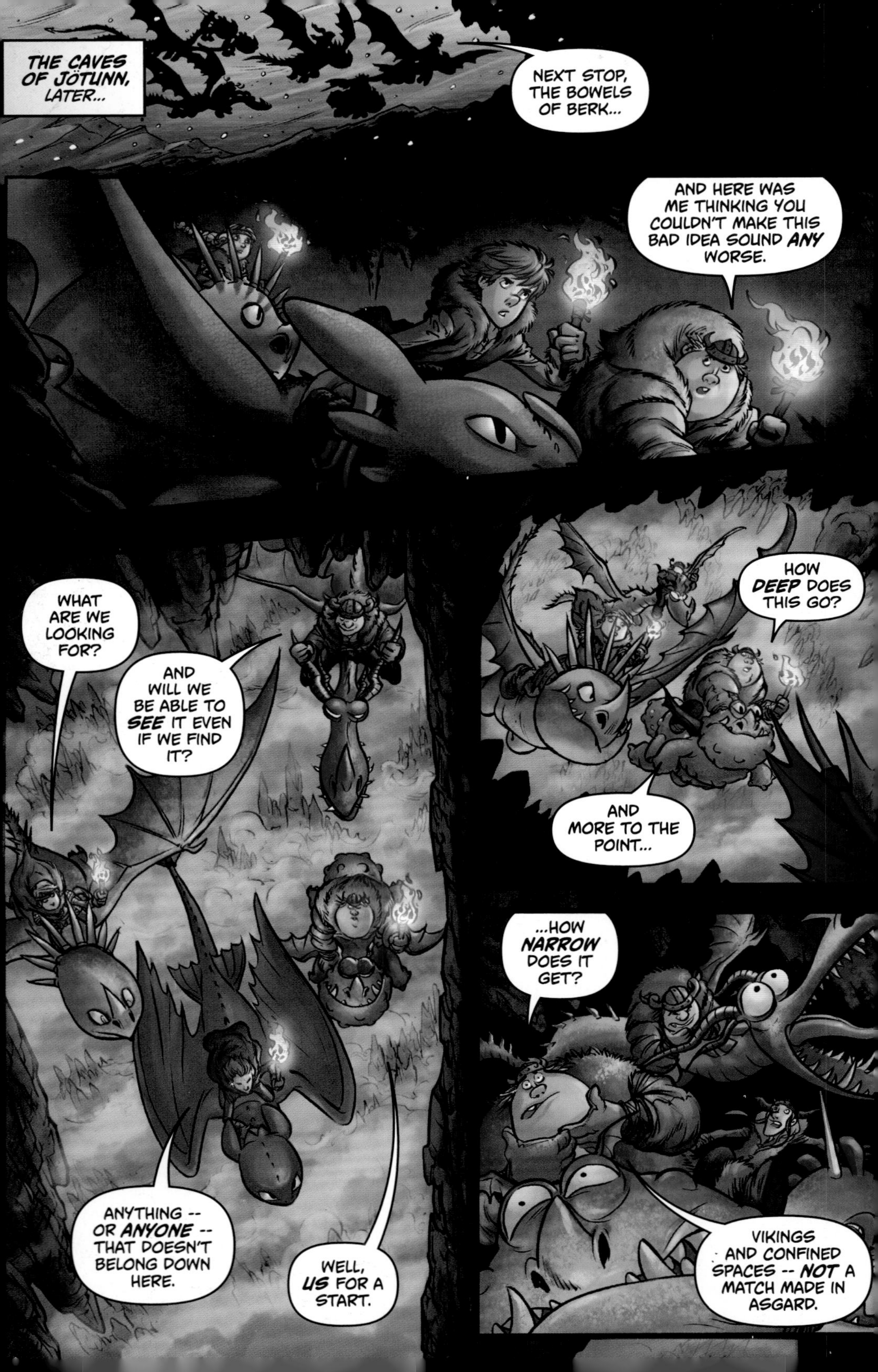
THE CAVES OF JÖTUNN, LATER...
NEXT STOP, THE BOWELS OF BERK...
AND HERE WAS ME THINKING YOU COULDN'T MAKE THIS BAD IDEA SOUND ANY WORSE.
WHAT ARE WE LOOKING FOR?
AND WILL WE BE ABLE TO SEE IT EVEN IF WE FIND IT?
ANYTHING -- OR ANYONE -- THAT DOESN'T BELONG DOWN HERE.
WELL, US FOR A START.
HOW DEEP DOES THIS GO?
AND MORE TO THE POINT...
...HOW NARROW DOES IT GET?
VIKINGS AND CONFINED SPACES -- NOT A MATCH MADE IN ASGARD.

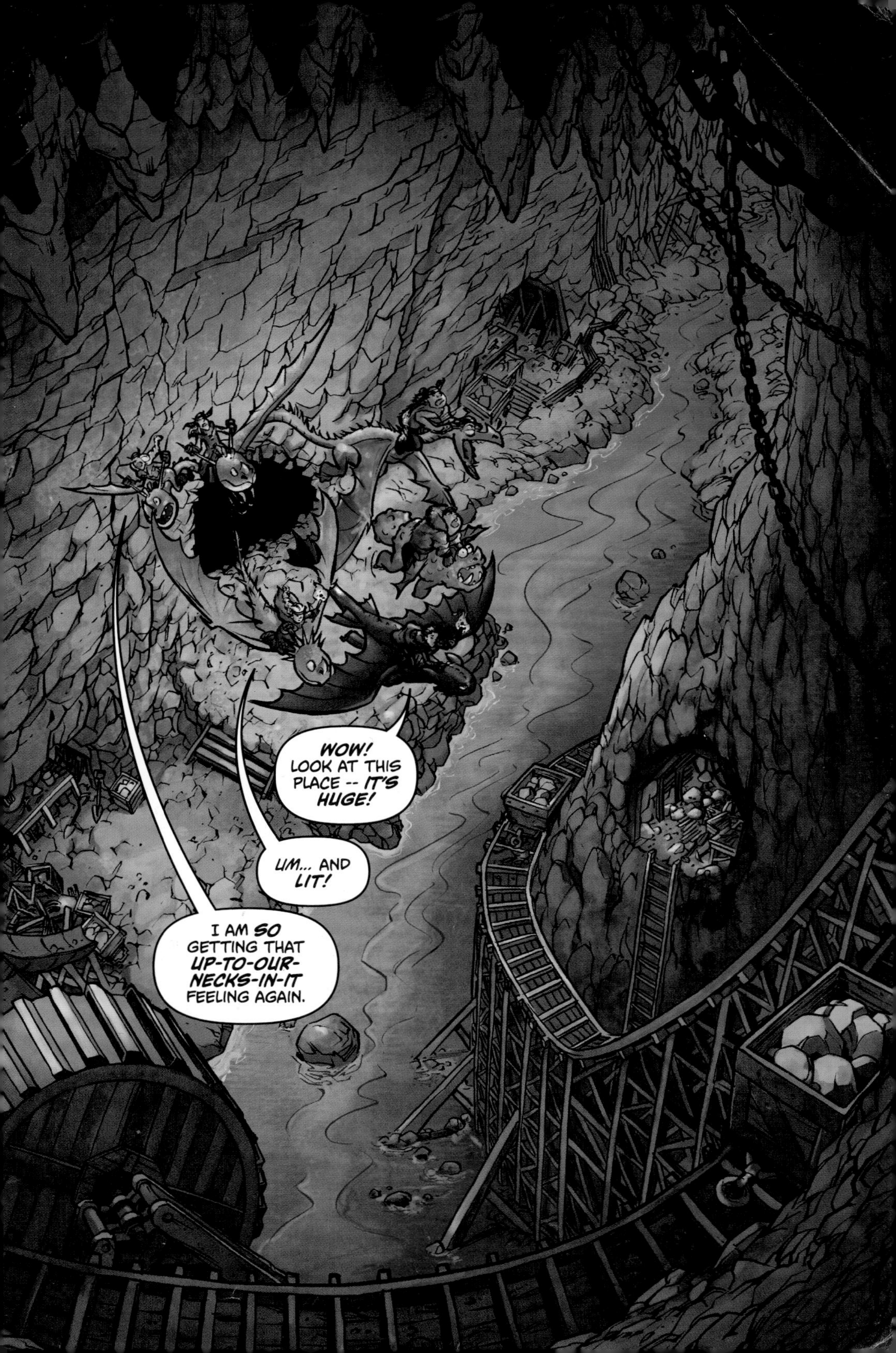
WOW! LOOK AT THIS PLACE -- IT'S HUGE!
UM... AND LIT!
I AM SO GETTING THAT UP-TO-OUR-NECKS-IN-IT FEELING AGAIN.

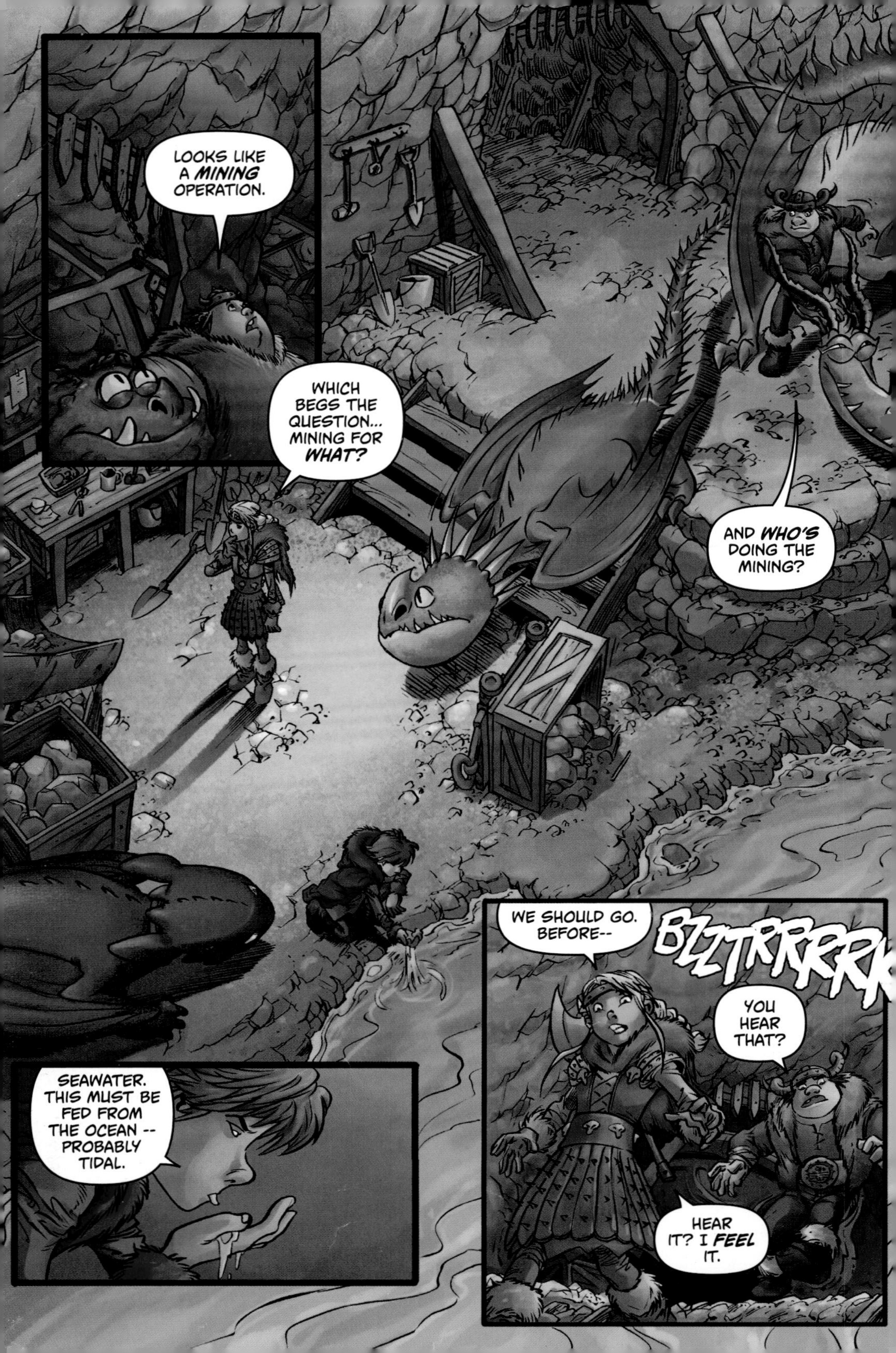
LOOKS LIKE A *MINING* OPERATION.
WHICH BEGS THE QUESTION... MINING FOR *WHAT?*
AND *WHO'S* DOING THE MINING?
SEAWATER. THIS MUST BE FED FROM THE OCEAN -- PROBABLY TIDAL.
WE SHOULD GO. BEFORE--
BZZTRRRRK
YOU HEAR THAT?
HEAR IT? I *FEEL* IT.

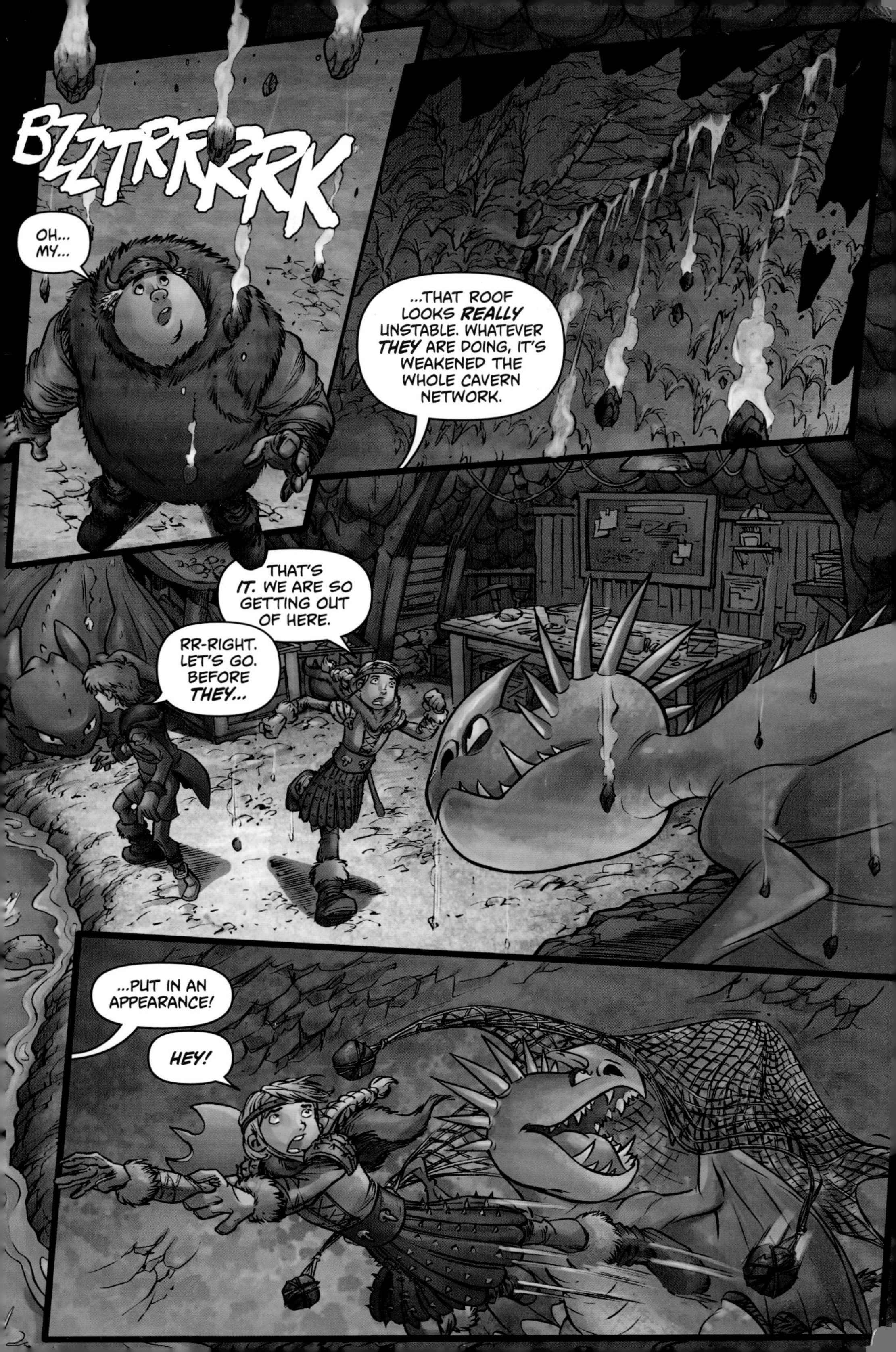
BZZTRRRRRK
OH... MY...
...THAT ROOF LOOKS REALLY UNSTABLE. WHATEVER THEY ARE DOING, IT'S WEAKENED THE WHOLE CAVERN NETWORK.
THAT'S IT. WE ARE SO GETTING OUT OF HERE.
RR-RIGHT. LET'S GO. BEFORE THEY...
...PUT IN AN APPEARANCE!
HEY!

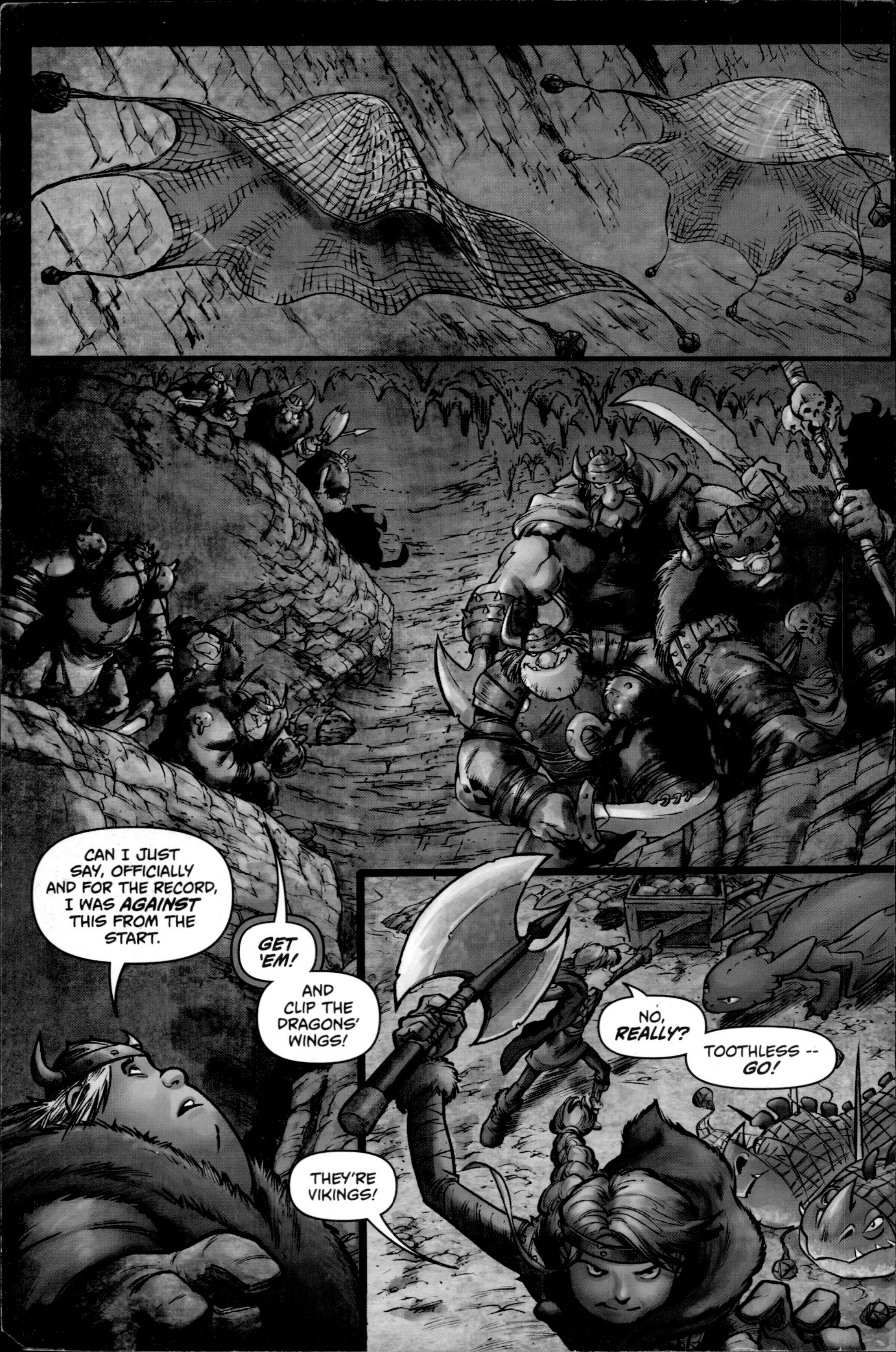
CAN I JUST SAY, OFFICIALLY AND FOR THE RECORD, I WAS *AGAINST* THIS FROM THE START.
GET 'EM!
AND CLIP THE DRAGONS' WINGS!
THEY'RE VIKINGS!
NO, *REALLY?*
TOOTHLESS -- *GO!*

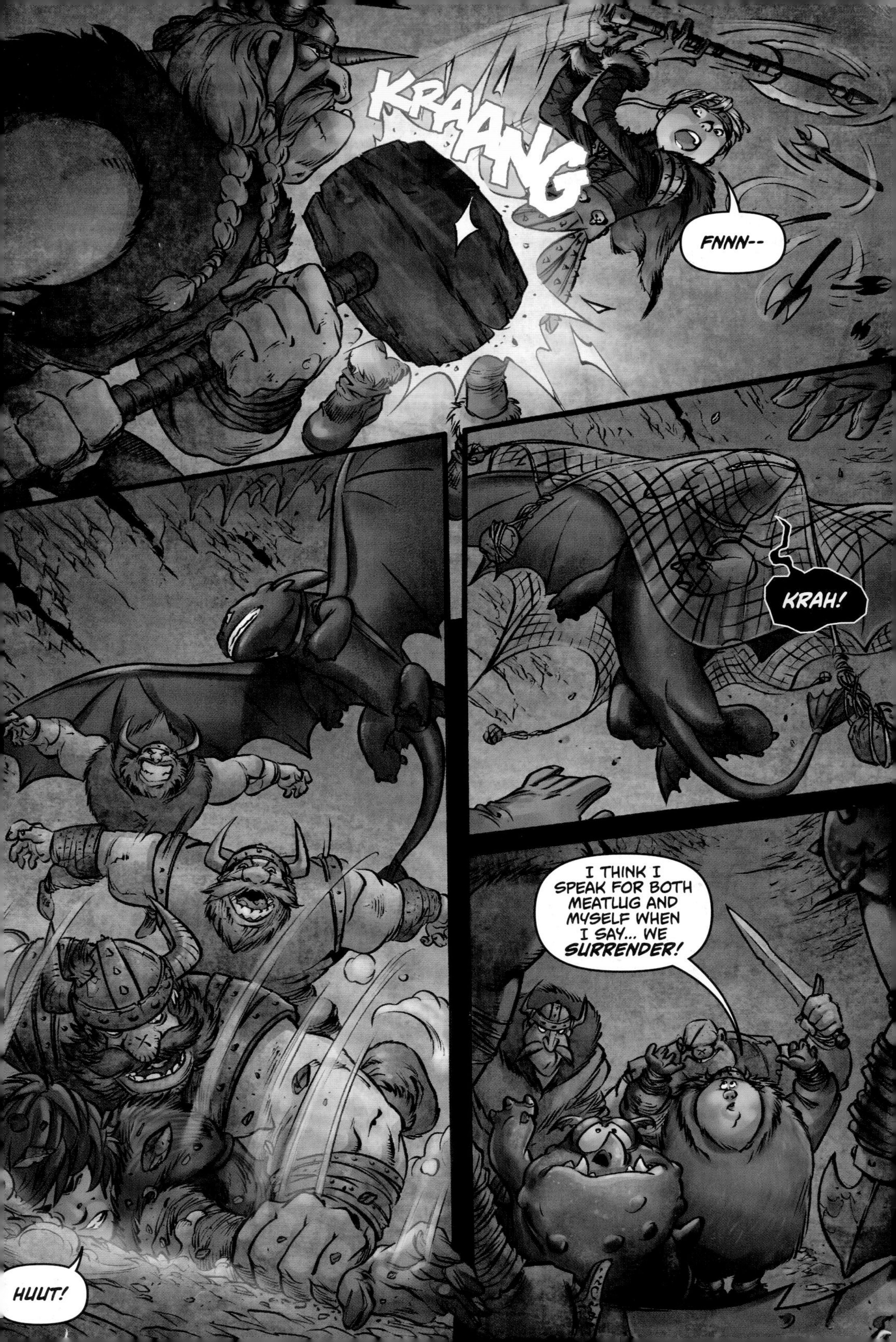
KRAANG
FNNN--
KRAH!
HUUT!
I THINK I SPEAK FOR BOTH MEATLUG AND MYSELF WHEN I SAY... WE SURRENDER!

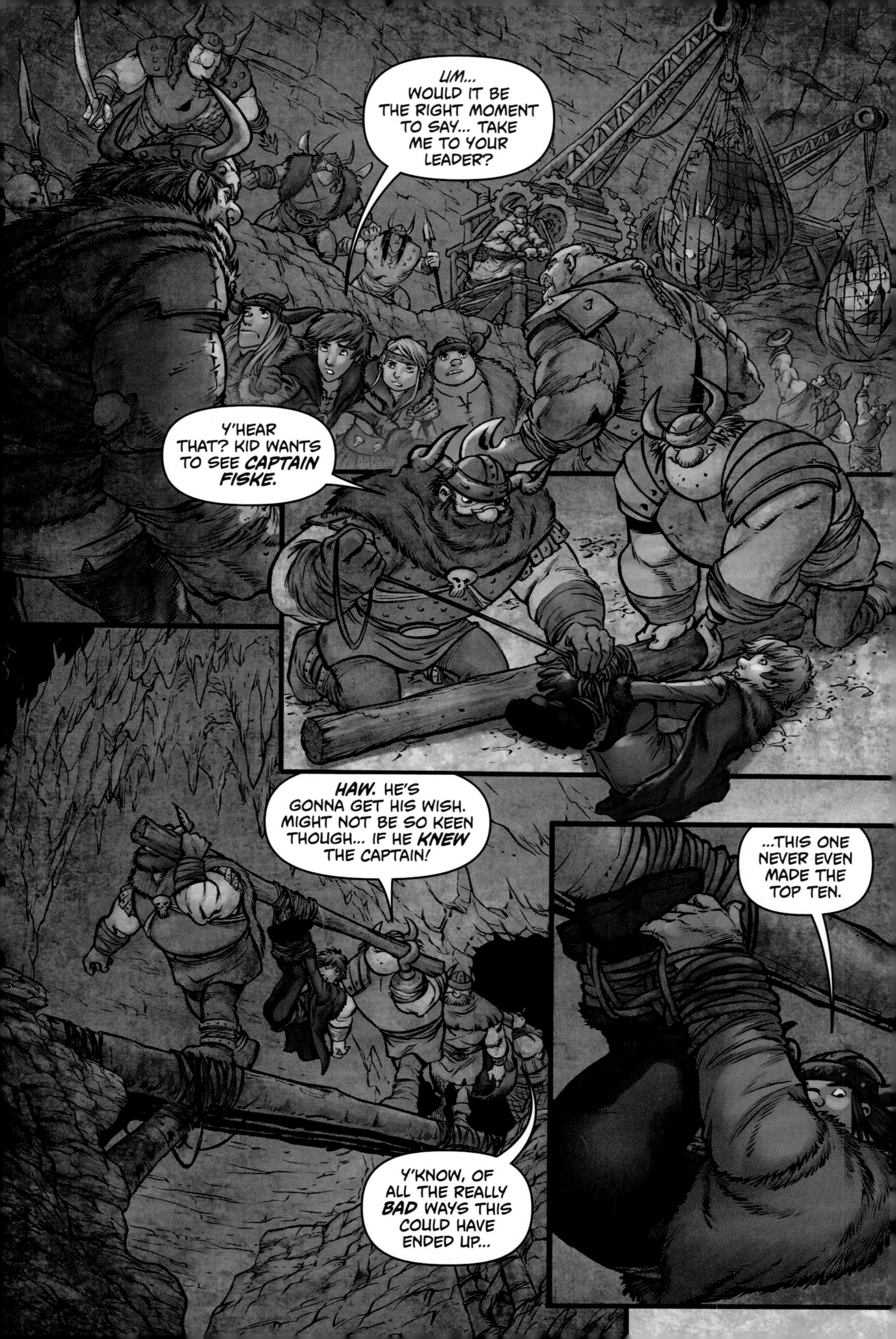
UM... WOULD IT BE THE RIGHT MOMENT TO SAY... TAKE ME TO YOUR LEADER?
Y'HEAR THAT? KID WANTS TO SEE CAPTAIN FISKE.
HAW. HE'S GONNA GET HIS WISH. MIGHT NOT BE SO KEEN THOUGH... IF HE KNEW THE CAPTAIN!
Y'KNOW, OF ALL THE REALLY BAD WAYS THIS COULD HAVE ENDED UP...
...THIS ONE NEVER EVEN MADE THE TOP TEN.

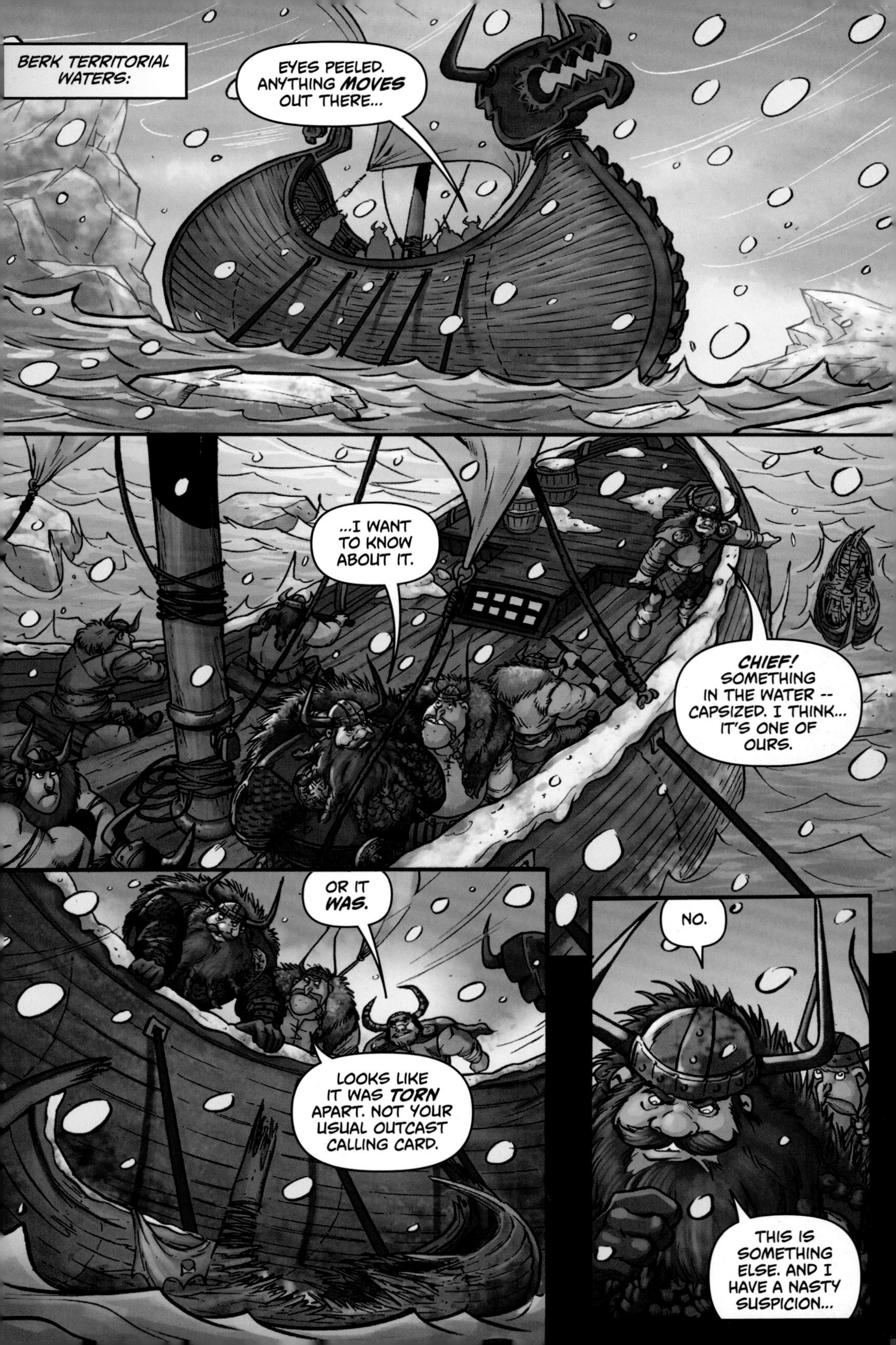
BERK TERRITORIAL WATERS:
EYES PEELED. ANYTHING MOVES OUT THERE...
...I WANT TO KNOW ABOUT IT.
CHIEF! SOMETHING IN THE WATER -- CAPSIZED. I THINK... IT'S ONE OF OURS.
OR IT WAS.
LOOKS LIKE IT WAS TORN APART. NOT YOUR USUAL OUTCAST CALLING CARD.
NO.
THIS IS SOMETHING ELSE. AND I HAVE A NASTY SUSPICION...

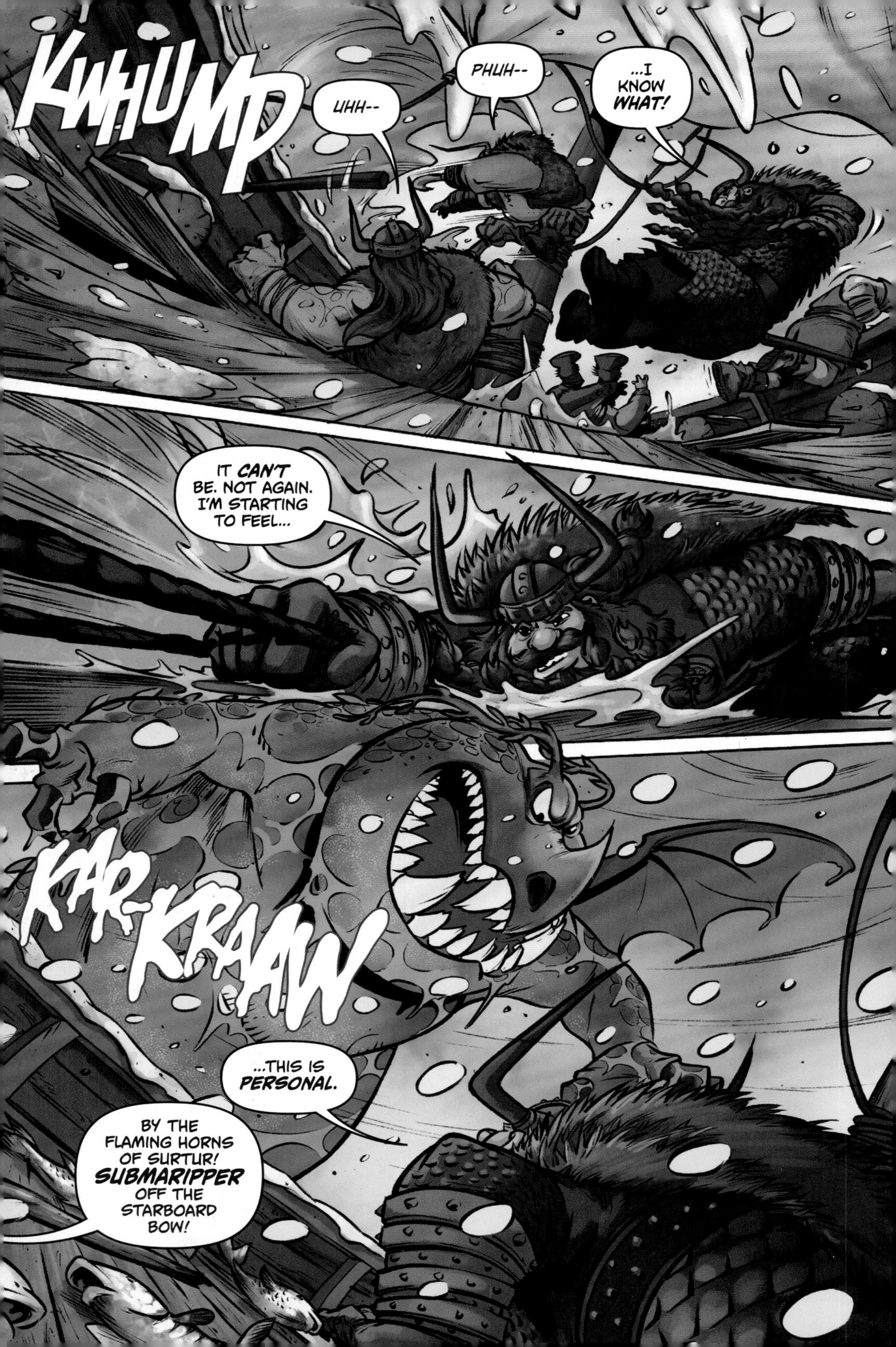
KWHUMP
UHH--
PHUH--
...I KNOW WHAT!
IT CAN'T BE. NOT AGAIN. I'M STARTING TO FEEL...
KAR-KRAAW
...THIS IS PERSONAL.
BY THE FLAMING HORNS OF SURTUR! SUBMARIPPER OFF THE STARBOARD BOW!

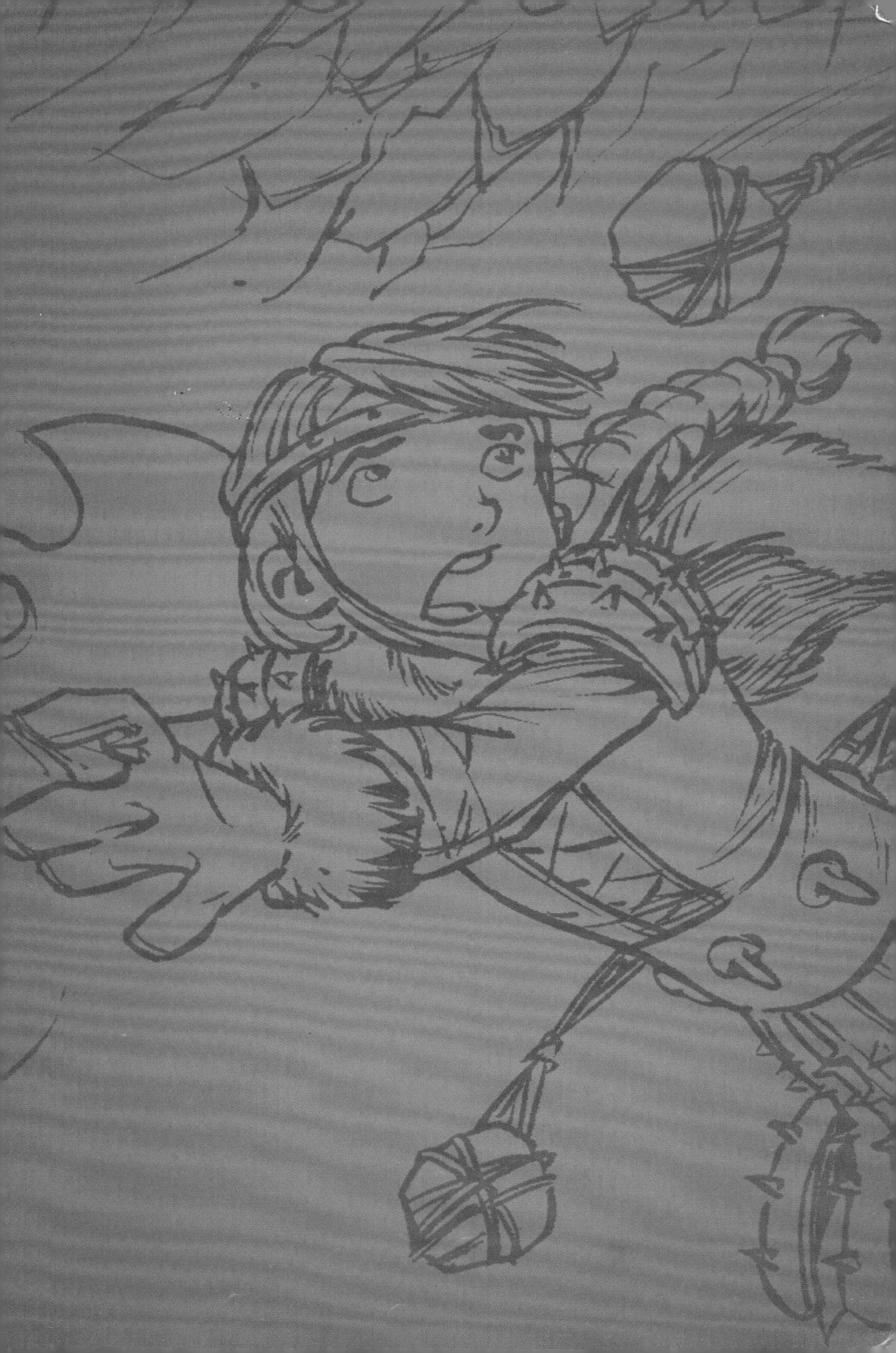

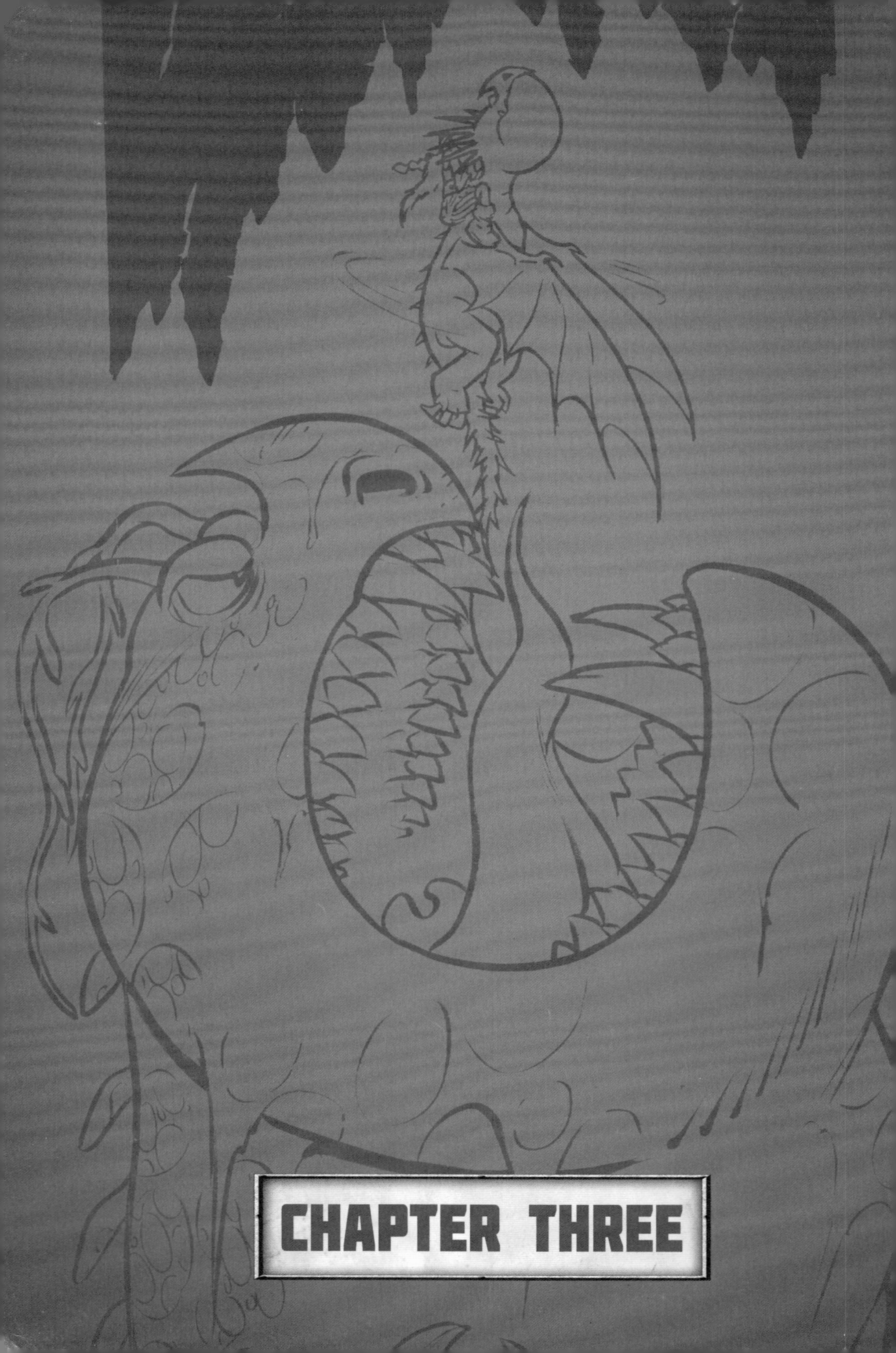

CHAPTER THREE

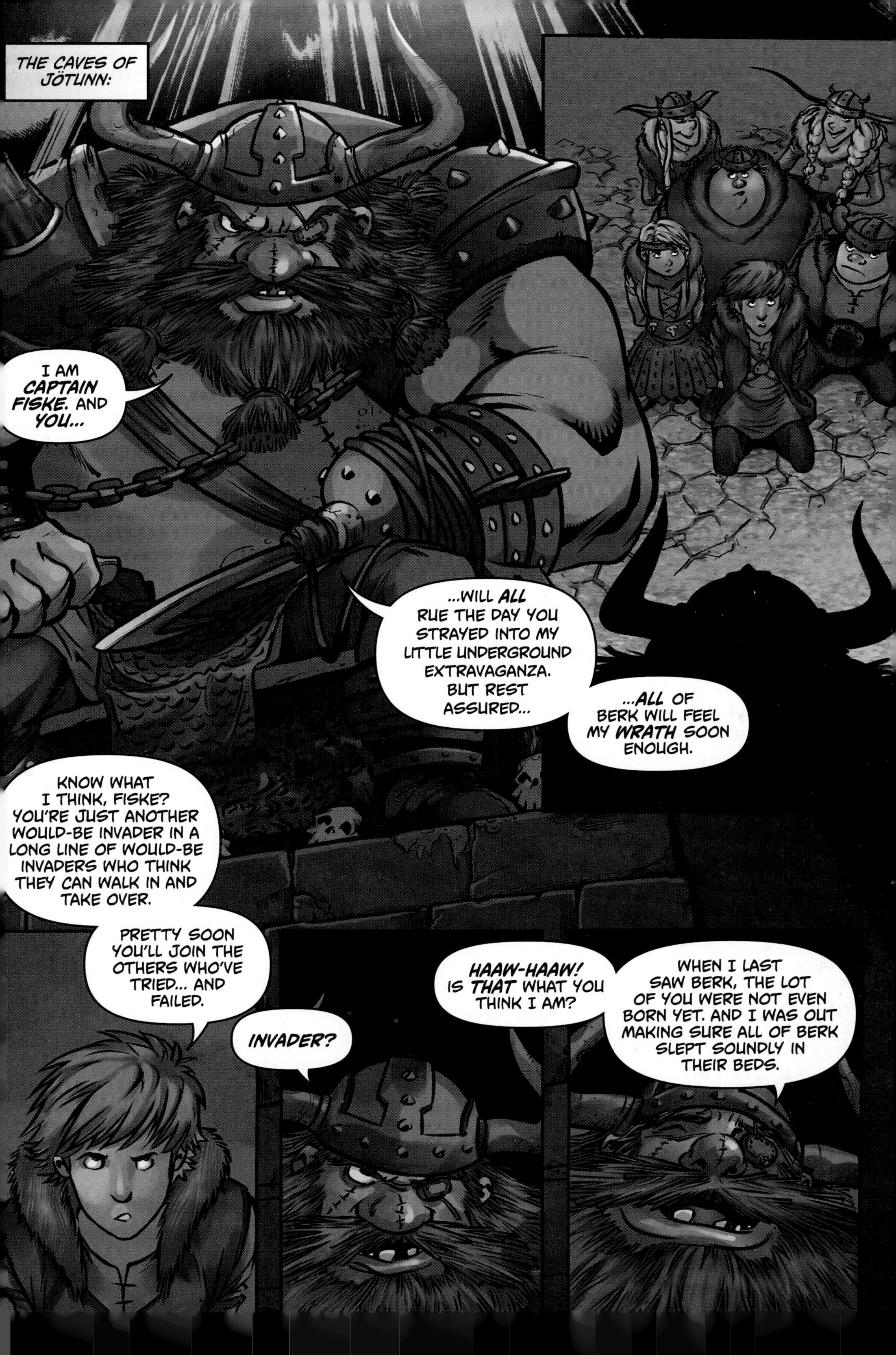
THE CAVES OF JÖTUNN:
I AM CAPTAIN FISKE. AND YOU...
...WILL ALL RUE THE DAY YOU STRAYED INTO MY LITTLE UNDERGROUND EXTRAVAGANZA. BUT REST ASSURED...
...ALL OF BERK WILL FEEL MY WRATH SOON ENOUGH.
KNOW WHAT I THINK, FISKE? YOU'RE JUST ANOTHER WOULD-BE INVADER IN A LONG LINE OF WOULD-BE INVADERS WHO THINK THEY CAN WALK IN AND TAKE OVER.
PRETTY SOON YOU'LL JOIN THE OTHERS WHO'VE TRIED... AND FAILED.
INVADER?
HAAW-HAAW! IS THAT WHAT YOU THINK I AM?
WHEN I LAST SAW BERK, THE LOT OF YOU WERE NOT EVEN BORN YET. AND I WAS OUT MAKING SURE ALL OF BERK SLEPT SOUNDLY IN THEIR BEDS.

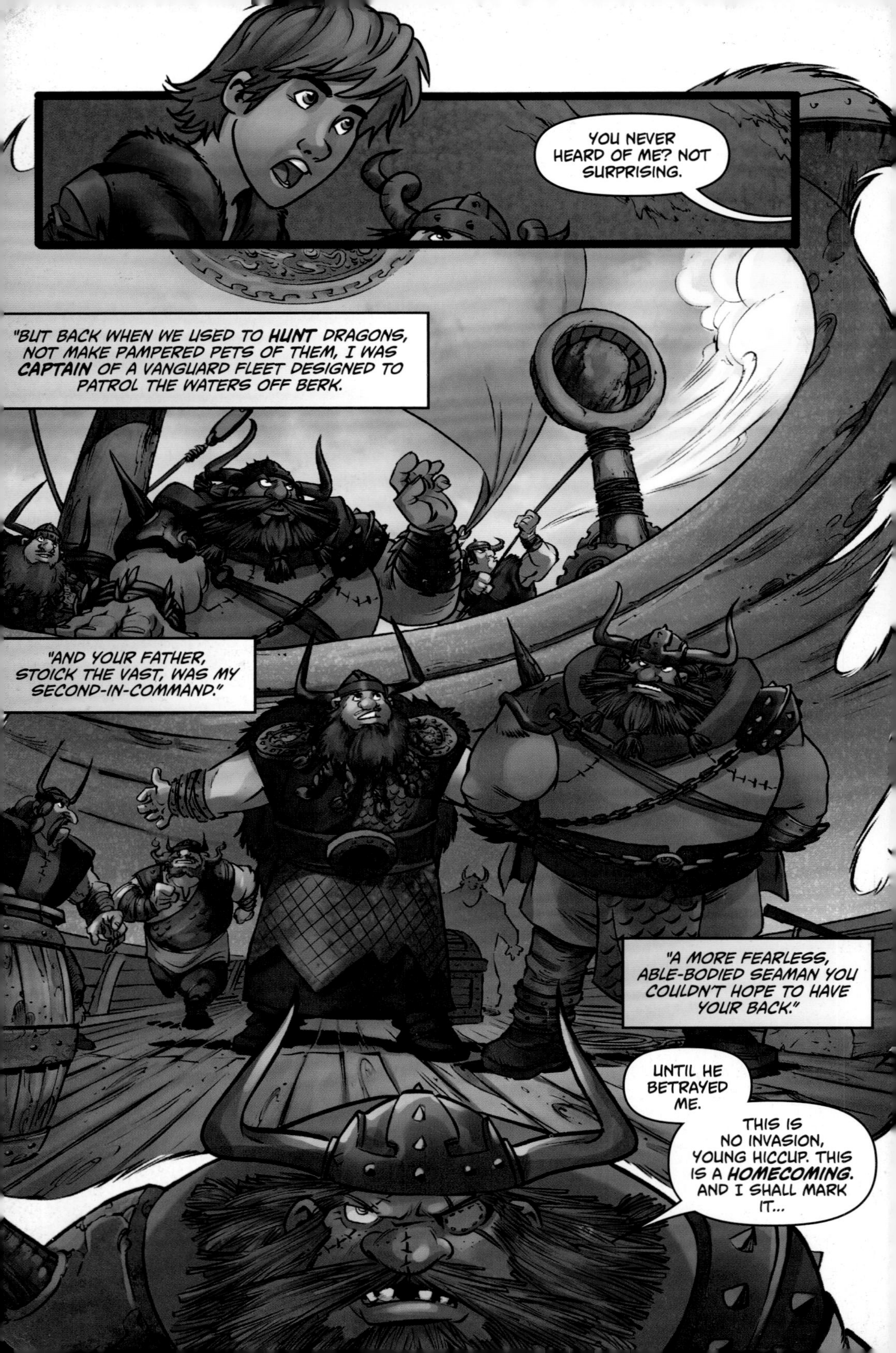
YOU NEVER HEARD OF ME? NOT SURPRISING.
"BUT BACK WHEN WE USED TO HUNT DRAGONS, NOT MAKE PAMPERED PETS OF THEM, I WAS CAPTAIN OF A VANGUARD FLEET DESIGNED TO PATROL THE WATERS OFF BERK.
"AND YOUR FATHER, STOICK THE VAST, WAS MY SECOND-IN-COMMAND."
"A MORE FEARLESS, ABLE-BODIED SEAMAN YOU COULDN'T HOPE TO HAVE YOUR BACK."
UNTIL HE BETRAYED ME.
THIS IS NO INVASION, YOUNG HICCUP. THIS IS A HOMECOMING. AND I SHALL MARK IT...

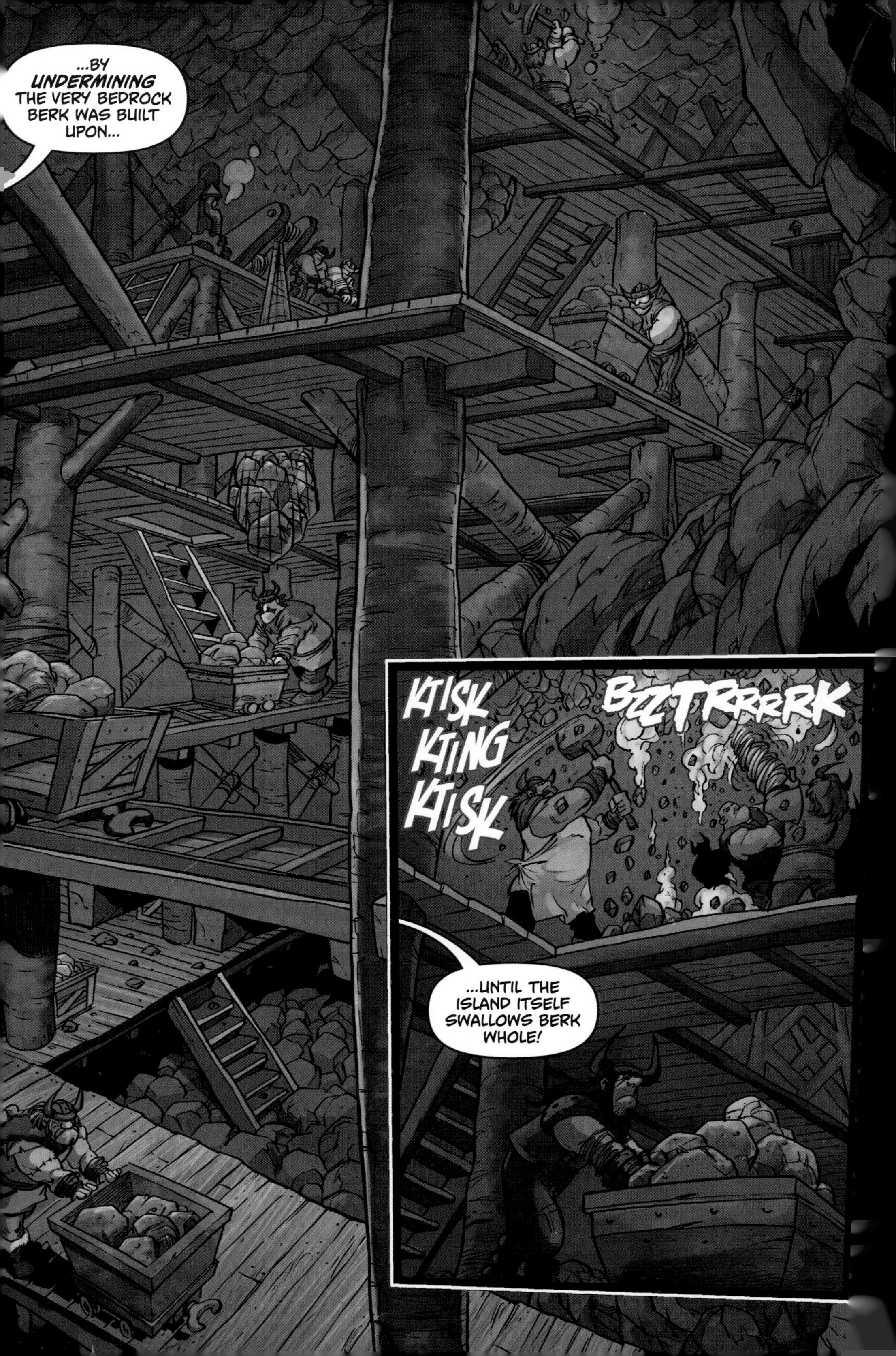
...BY UNDERMINING THE VERY BEDROCK BERK WAS BUILT UPON...
KTISK
KTING
KTISK
BZZTRRRRK
...UNTIL THE ISLAND ITSELF SWALLOWS BERK WHOLE!

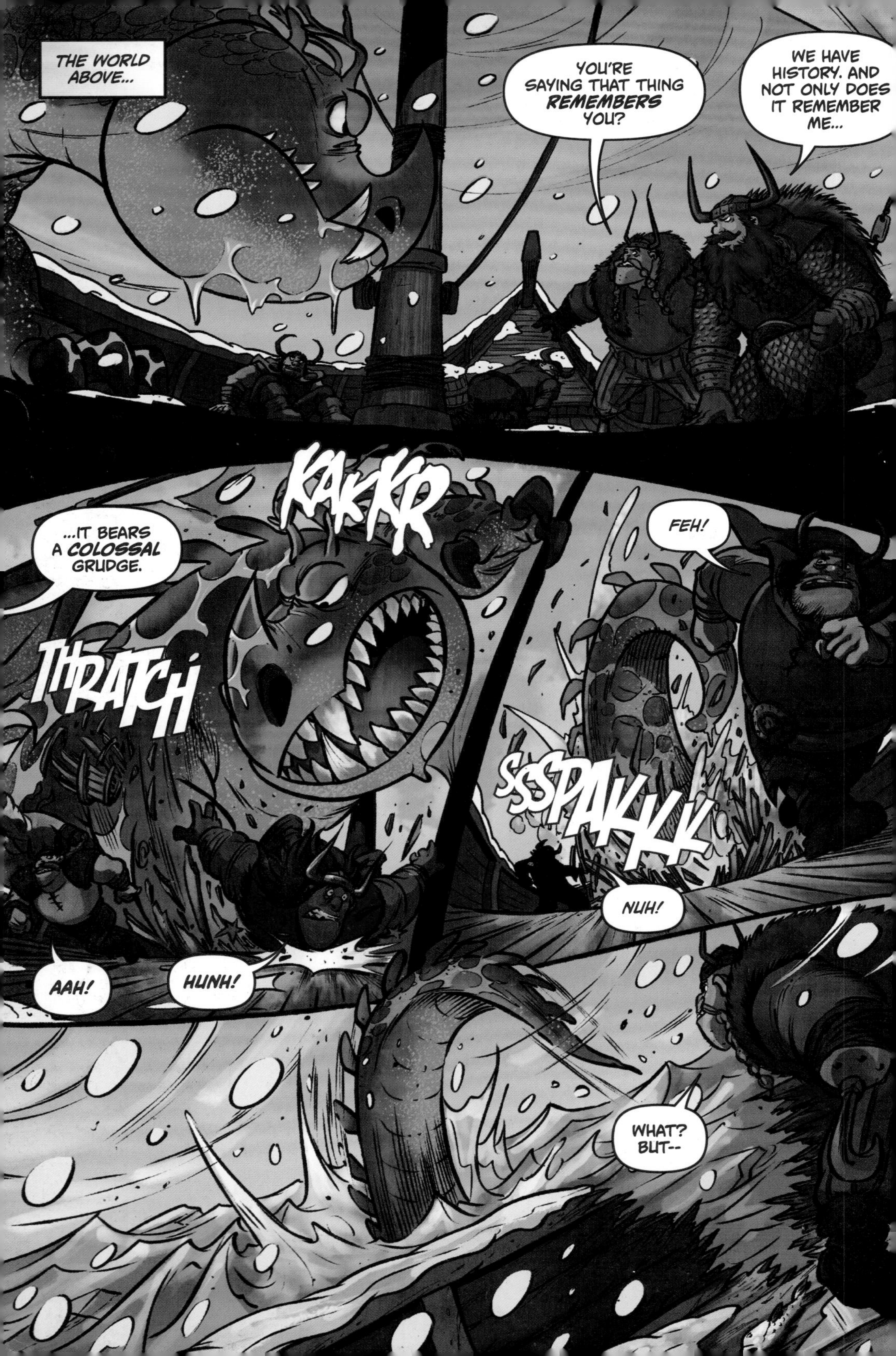
THE WORLD ABOVE...
YOU'RE SAYING THAT THING *REMEMBERS* YOU?
WE HAVE HISTORY. AND NOT ONLY DOES IT REMEMBER ME...
KAKKR
...IT BEARS A *COLOSSAL* GRUDGE.
THRATCH
FEH!
SSSPAKKK
NUH!
AAH!
HUNH!
WHAT? BUT--

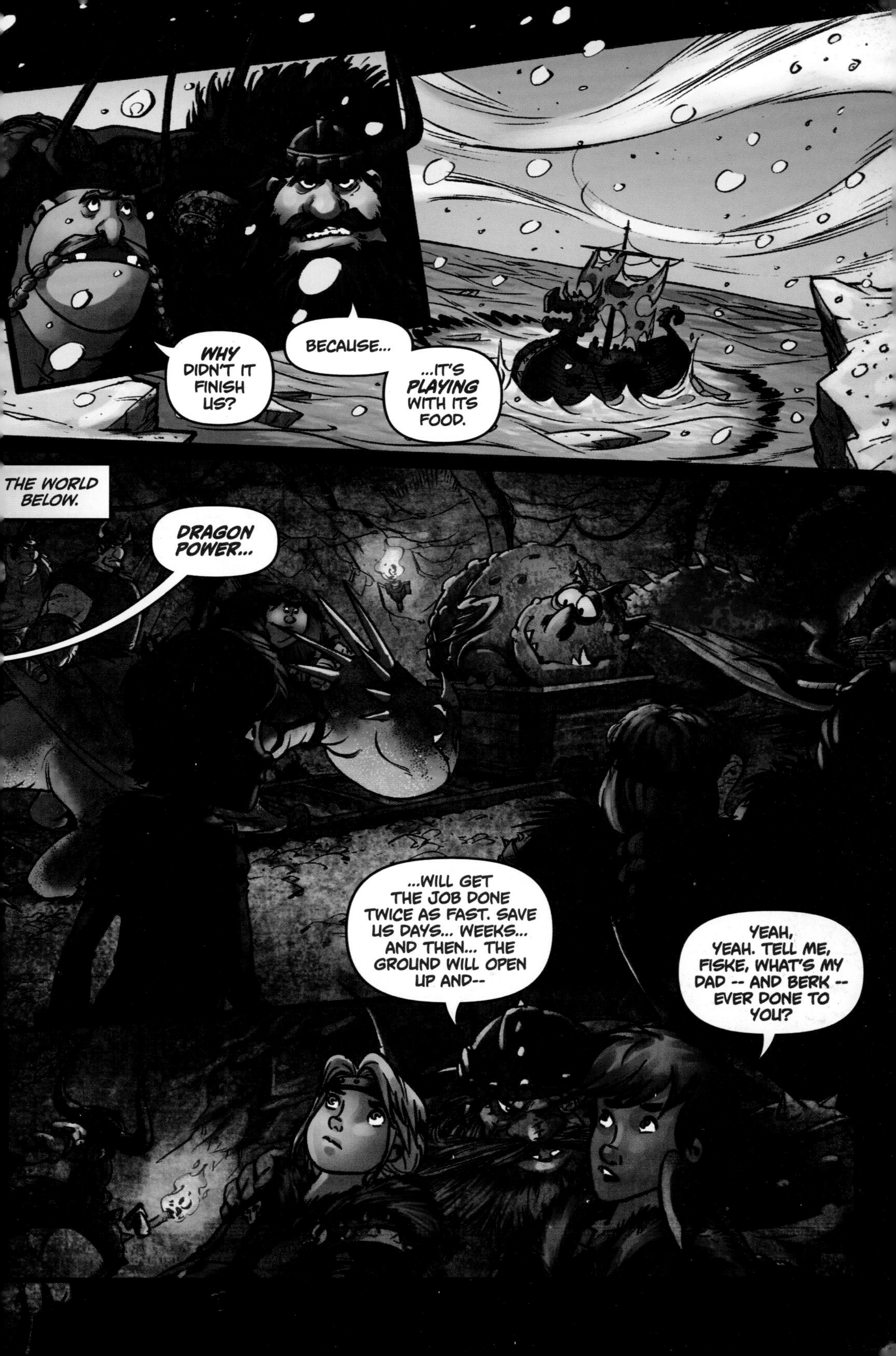
WHY DIDN'T IT FINISH US?
BECAUSE...
...IT'S PLAYING WITH ITS FOOD.
THE WORLD BELOW.
DRAGON POWER...
...WILL GET THE JOB DONE TWICE AS FAST. SAVE US DAYS... WEEKS... AND THEN... THE GROUND WILL OPEN UP AND--
YEAH, YEAH. TELL ME, FISKE, WHAT'S MY DAD -- AND BERK -- EVER DONE TO YOU?

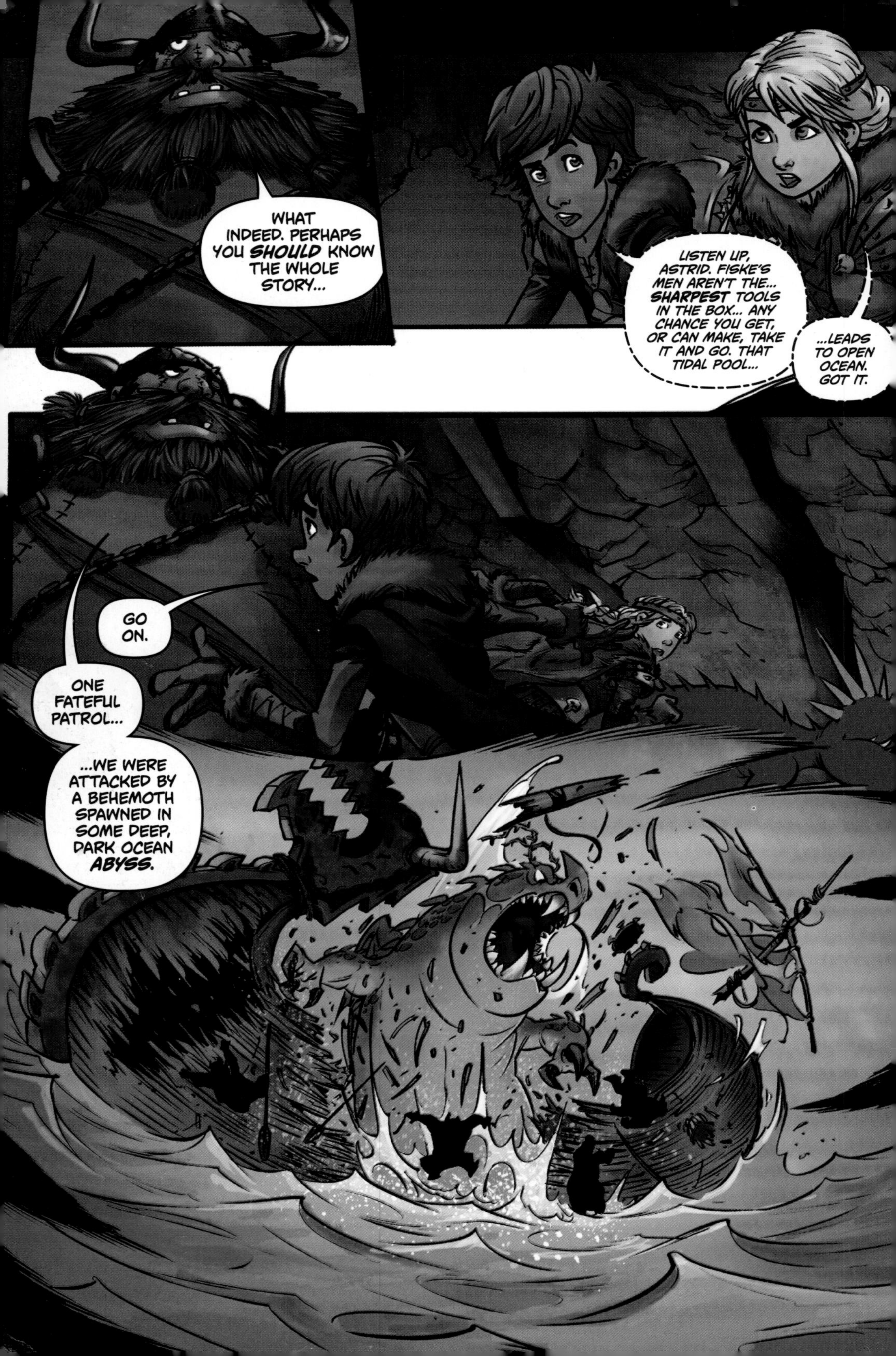
WHAT INDEED. PERHAPS YOU **SHOULD** KNOW THE WHOLE STORY...
LISTEN UP, ASTRID. FISKE'S MEN AREN'T THE... **SHARPEST** TOOLS IN THE BOX... ANY CHANCE YOU GET, OR CAN MAKE, TAKE IT AND GO. THAT TIDAL POOL...
...LEADS TO OPEN OCEAN. GOT IT.
GO ON.
ONE FATEFUL PATROL...
...WE WERE ATTACKED BY A BEHEMOTH SPAWNED IN SOME DEEP, DARK OCEAN **ABYSS**.

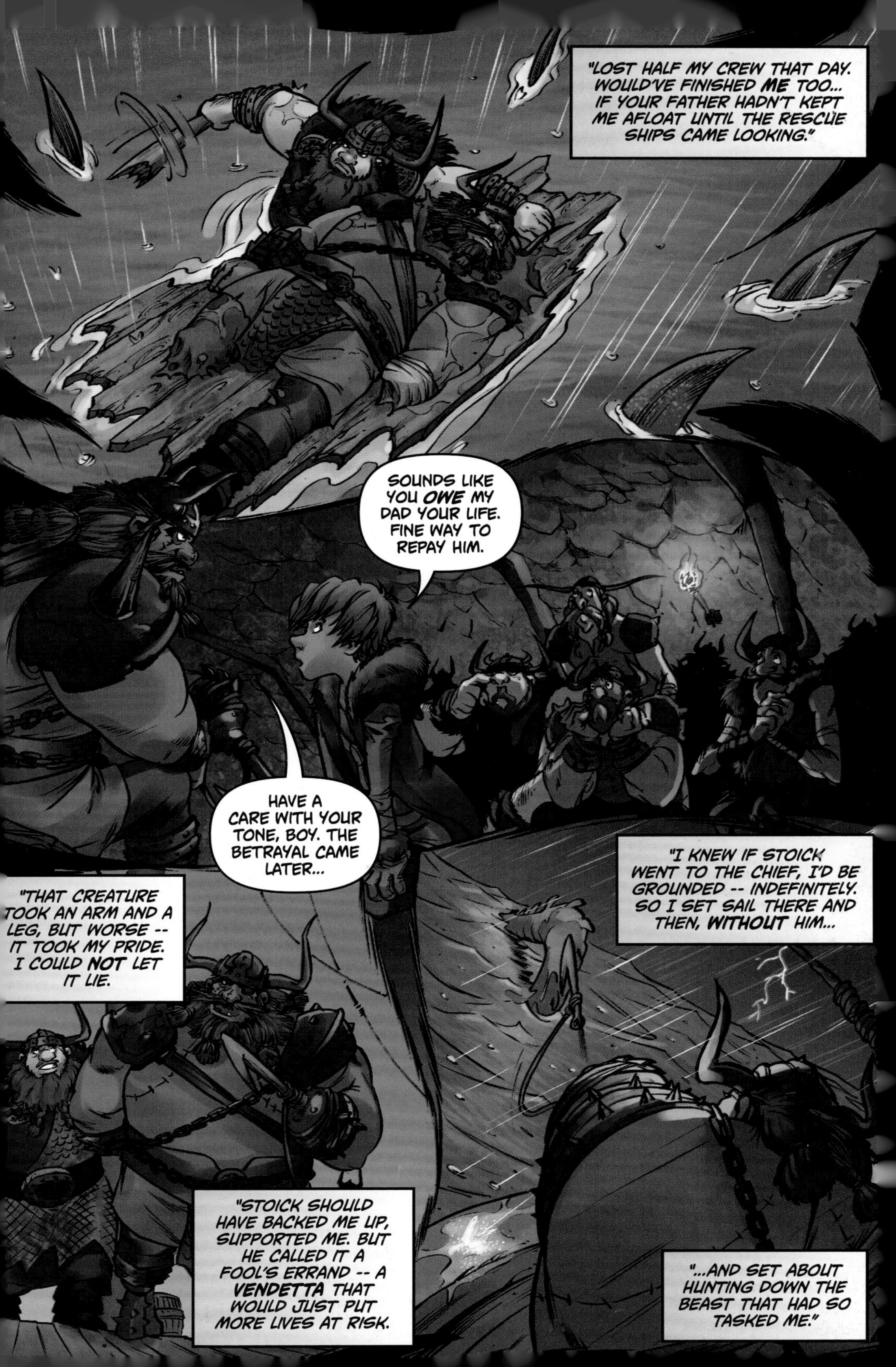
"LOST HALF MY CREW THAT DAY. WOULD'VE FINISHED ME TOO... IF YOUR FATHER HADN'T KEPT ME AFLOAT UNTIL THE RESCUE SHIPS CAME LOOKING."
SOUNDS LIKE YOU OWE MY DAD YOUR LIFE. FINE WAY TO REPAY HIM.
HAVE A CARE WITH YOUR TONE, BOY. THE BETRAYAL CAME LATER...
"THAT CREATURE TOOK AN ARM AND A LEG, BUT WORSE -- IT TOOK MY PRIDE. I COULD NOT LET IT LIE.
"STOICK SHOULD HAVE BACKED ME UP, SUPPORTED ME. BUT HE CALLED IT A FOOL'S ERRAND -- A VENDETTA THAT WOULD JUST PUT MORE LIVES AT RISK.
"I KNEW IF STOICK WENT TO THE CHIEF, I'D BE GROUNDED -- INDEFINITELY. SO I SET SAIL THERE AND THEN, WITHOUT HIM...
"...AND SET ABOUT HUNTING DOWN THE BEAST THAT HAD SO TASKED ME."

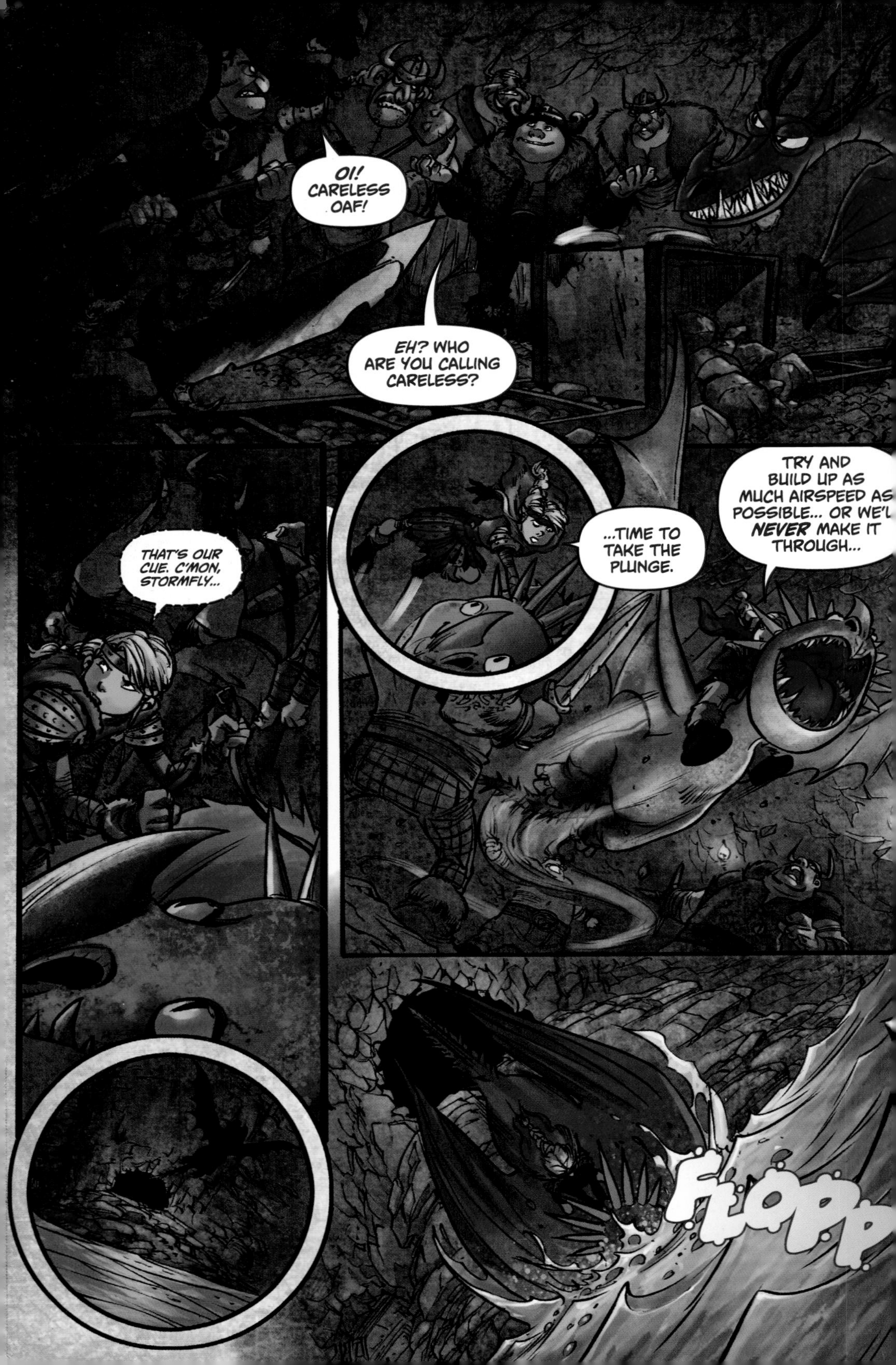
OI! CARELESS OAF!
EH? WHO ARE YOU CALLING CARELESS?
THAT'S OUR CUE. C'MON, STORMFLY...
...TIME TO TAKE THE PLUNGE.
TRY AND BUILD UP AS MUCH AIRSPEED AS POSSIBLE... OR WE'LL NEVER MAKE IT THROUGH...
FLOPP

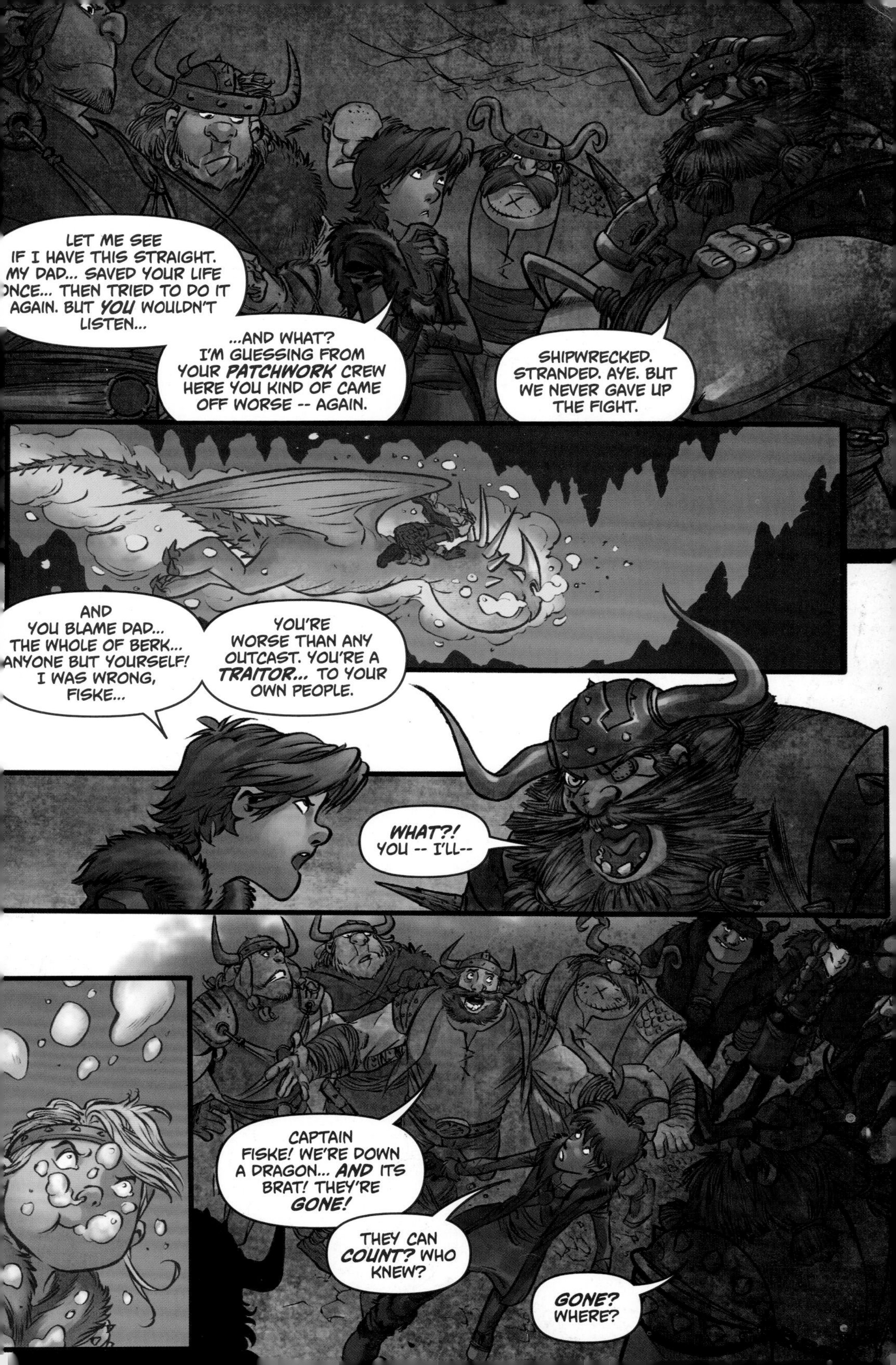
LET ME SEE IF I HAVE THIS STRAIGHT. MY DAD... SAVED YOUR LIFE ONCE... THEN TRIED TO DO IT AGAIN. BUT YOU WOULDN'T LISTEN...
...AND WHAT? I'M GUESSING FROM YOUR PATCHWORK CREW HERE YOU KIND OF CAME OFF WORSE -- AGAIN.
SHIPWRECKED. STRANDED. AYE. BUT WE NEVER GAVE UP THE FIGHT.
AND YOU BLAME DAD... THE WHOLE OF BERK... ANYONE BUT YOURSELF! I WAS WRONG, FISKE...
YOU'RE WORSE THAN ANY OUTCAST. YOU'RE A TRAITOR... TO YOUR OWN PEOPLE.
WHAT?! YOU -- I'LL--
CAPTAIN FISKE! WE'RE DOWN A DRAGON... AND ITS BRAT! THEY'RE GONE!
THEY CAN COUNT? WHO KNEW?
GONE? WHERE?

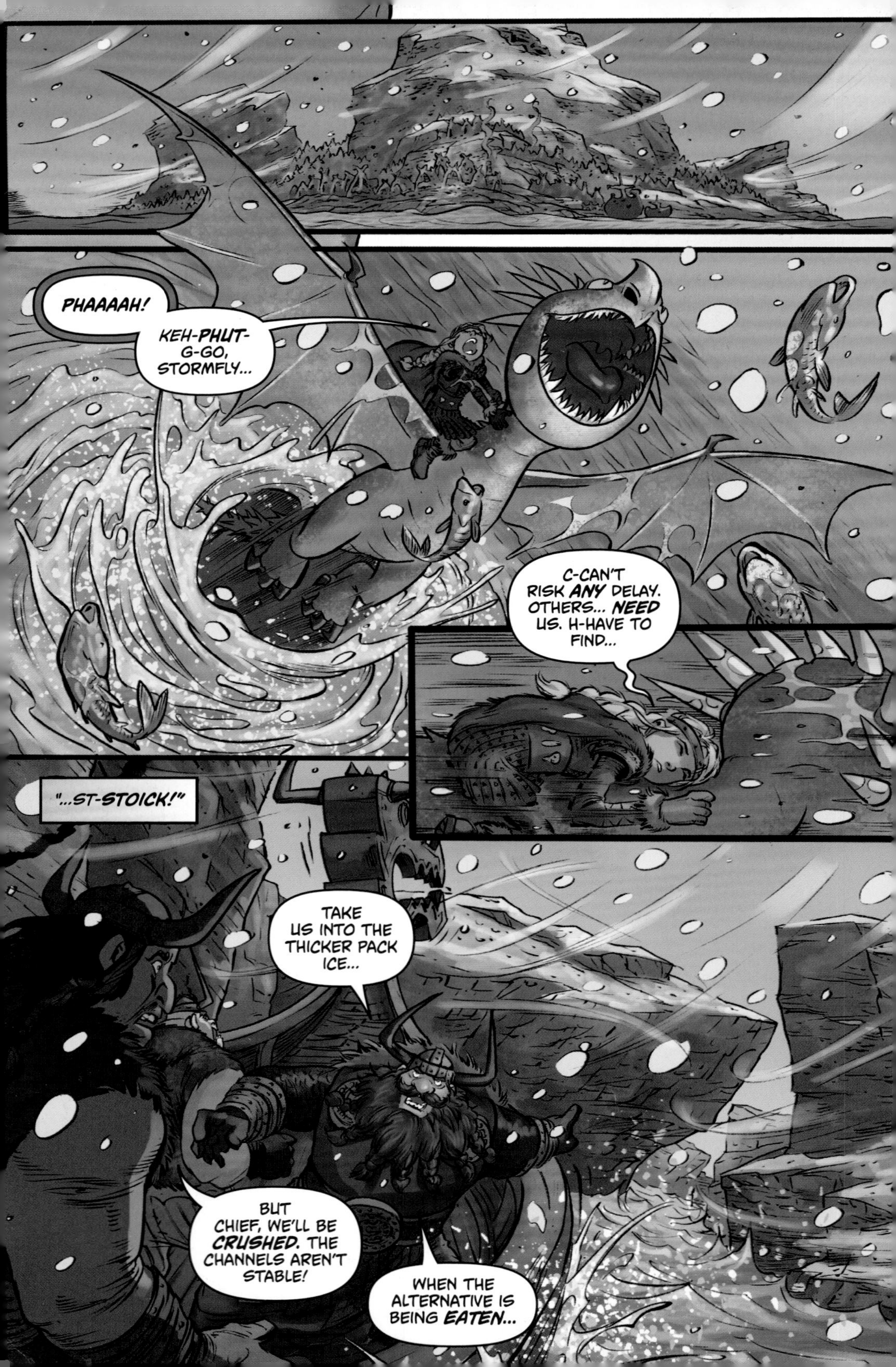
PHAAAAH!
KEH-PHUT-G-GO, STORMFLY...
C-CAN'T RISK ANY DELAY. OTHERS... NEED US. H-HAVE TO FIND...
"...ST-STOICK!"
TAKE US INTO THE THICKER PACK ICE...
BUT CHIEF, WE'LL BE CRUSHED. THE CHANNELS AREN'T STABLE!
WHEN THE ALTERNATIVE IS BEING EATEN...

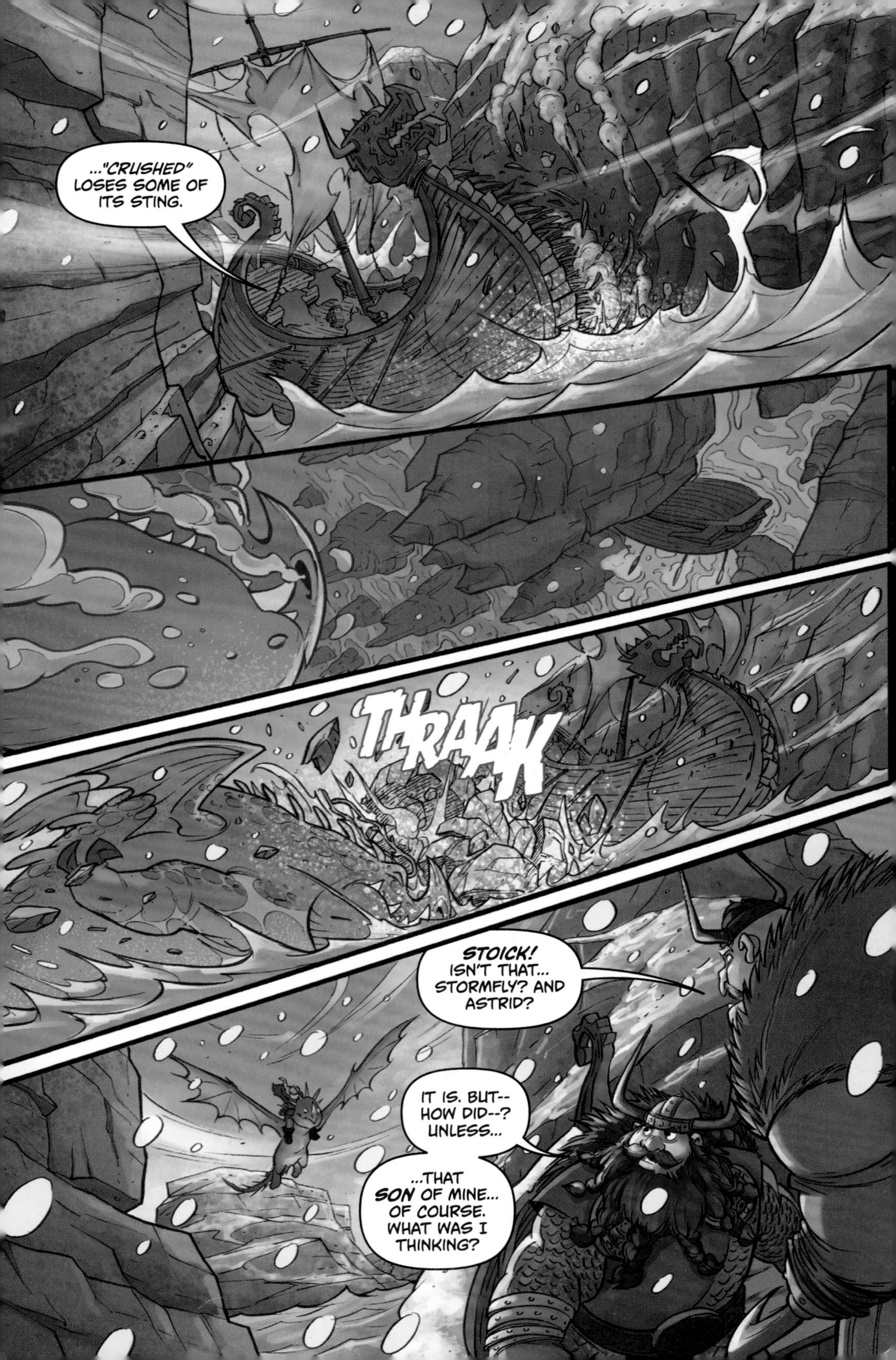
..."CRUSHED" LOSES SOME OF ITS STING.
THRAAK
STOICK! ISN'T THAT... STORMFLY? AND ASTRID?
IT IS. BUT-- HOW DID--? UNLESS...
...THAT SON OF MINE... OF COURSE. WHAT WAS I THINKING?

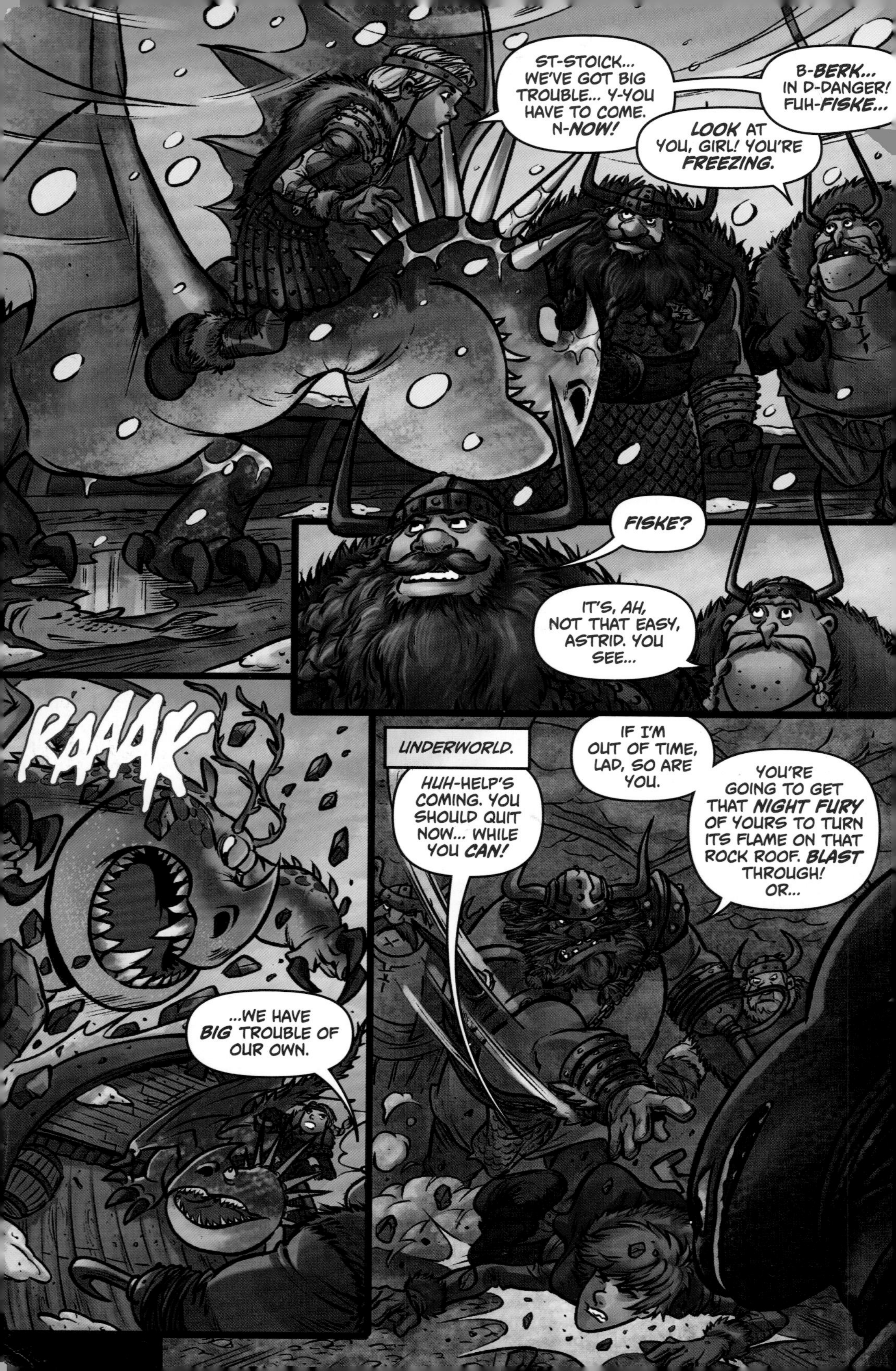
ST-STOICK... WE'VE GOT BIG TROUBLE... Y-YOU HAVE TO COME. N-NOW!
B-BERK... IN D-DANGER! FUH-FISKE...
LOOK AT YOU, GIRL! YOU'RE FREEZING.
FISKE?
IT'S, AH, NOT THAT EASY, ASTRID. YOU SEE...
RAAAK
...WE HAVE BIG TROUBLE OF OUR OWN.
UNDERWORLD.
HUH-HELP'S COMING. YOU SHOULD QUIT NOW... WHILE YOU CAN!
IF I'M OUT OF TIME, LAD, SO ARE YOU.
YOU'RE GOING TO GET THAT NIGHT FURY OF YOURS TO TURN ITS FLAME ON THAT ROCK ROOF. BLAST THROUGH! OR...

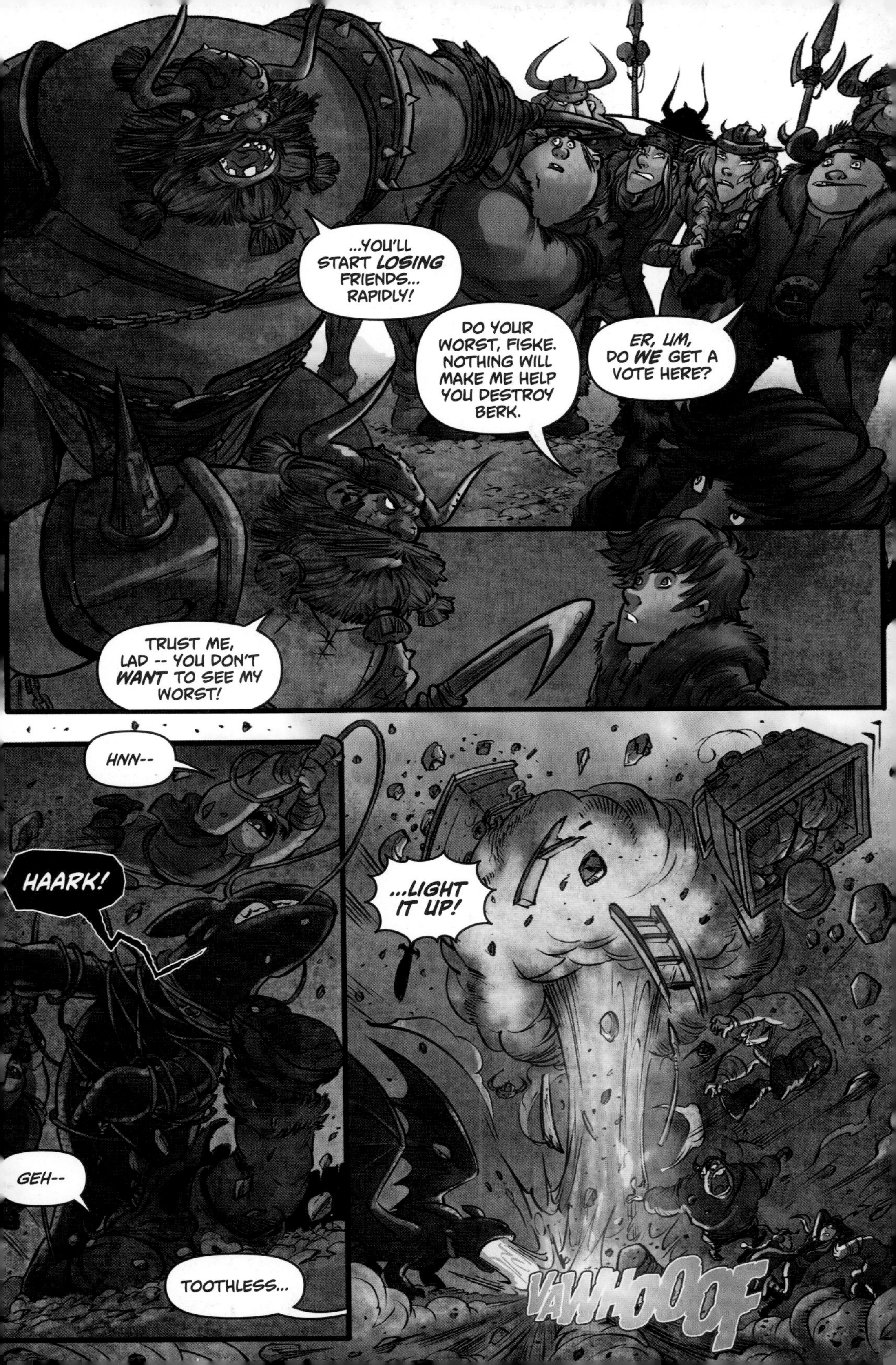

...YOU'LL START LOSING FRIENDS... RAPIDLY!
DO YOUR WORST, FISKE. NOTHING WILL MAKE ME HELP YOU DESTROY BERK.
ER, UM, DO WE GET A VOTE HERE?
TRUST ME, LAD -- YOU DON'T WANT TO SEE MY WORST!
HNN--
HAARK!
GEH--
TOOTHLESS...
...LIGHT IT UP!
VAWHOOOF

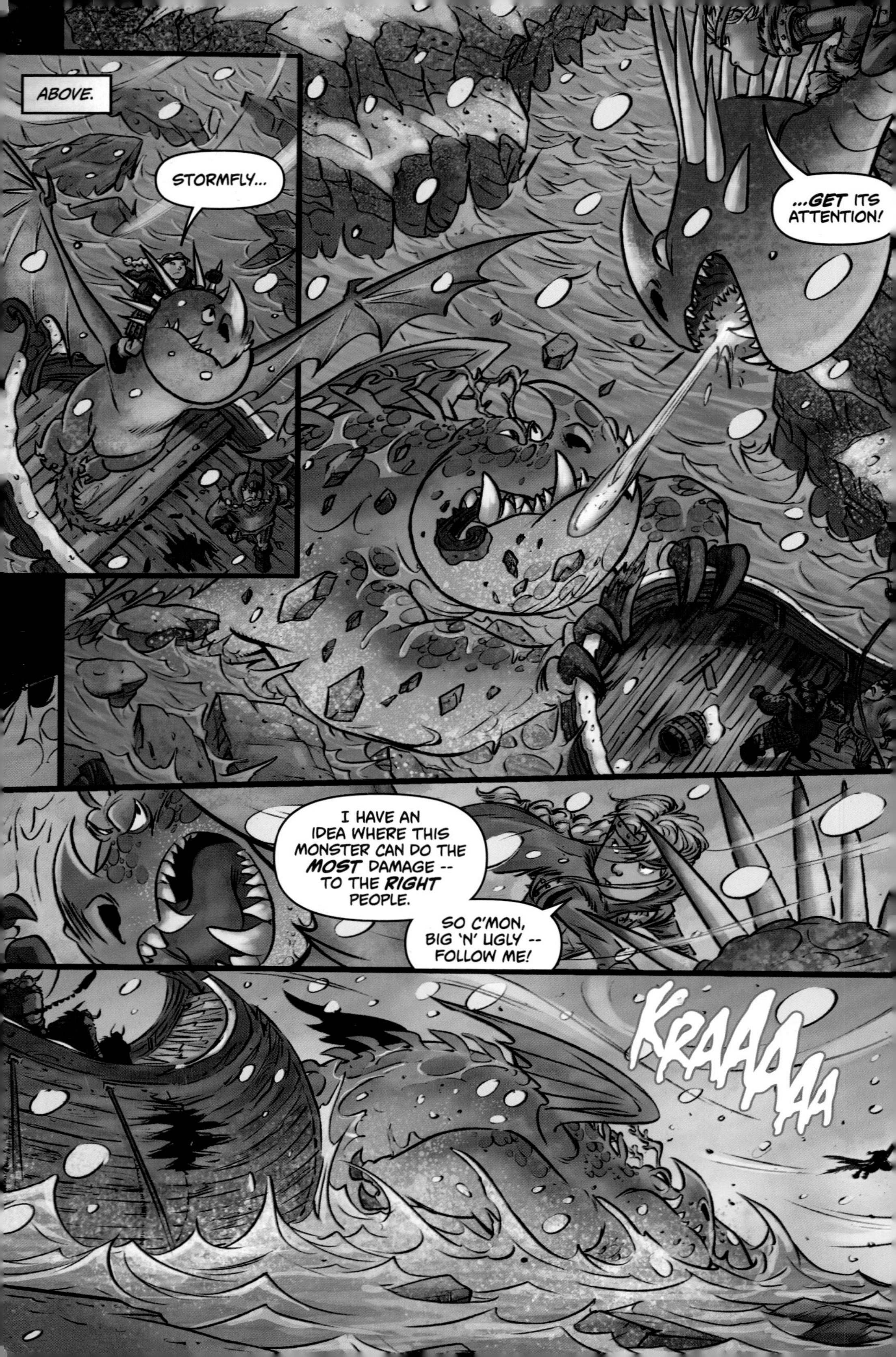
ABOVE.
STORMFLY...
...GET ITS ATTENTION!
I HAVE AN IDEA WHERE THIS MONSTER CAN DO THE MOST DAMAGE -- TO THE RIGHT PEOPLE.
SO C'MON, BIG 'N' UGLY -- FOLLOW ME!
KRAAAAAAA

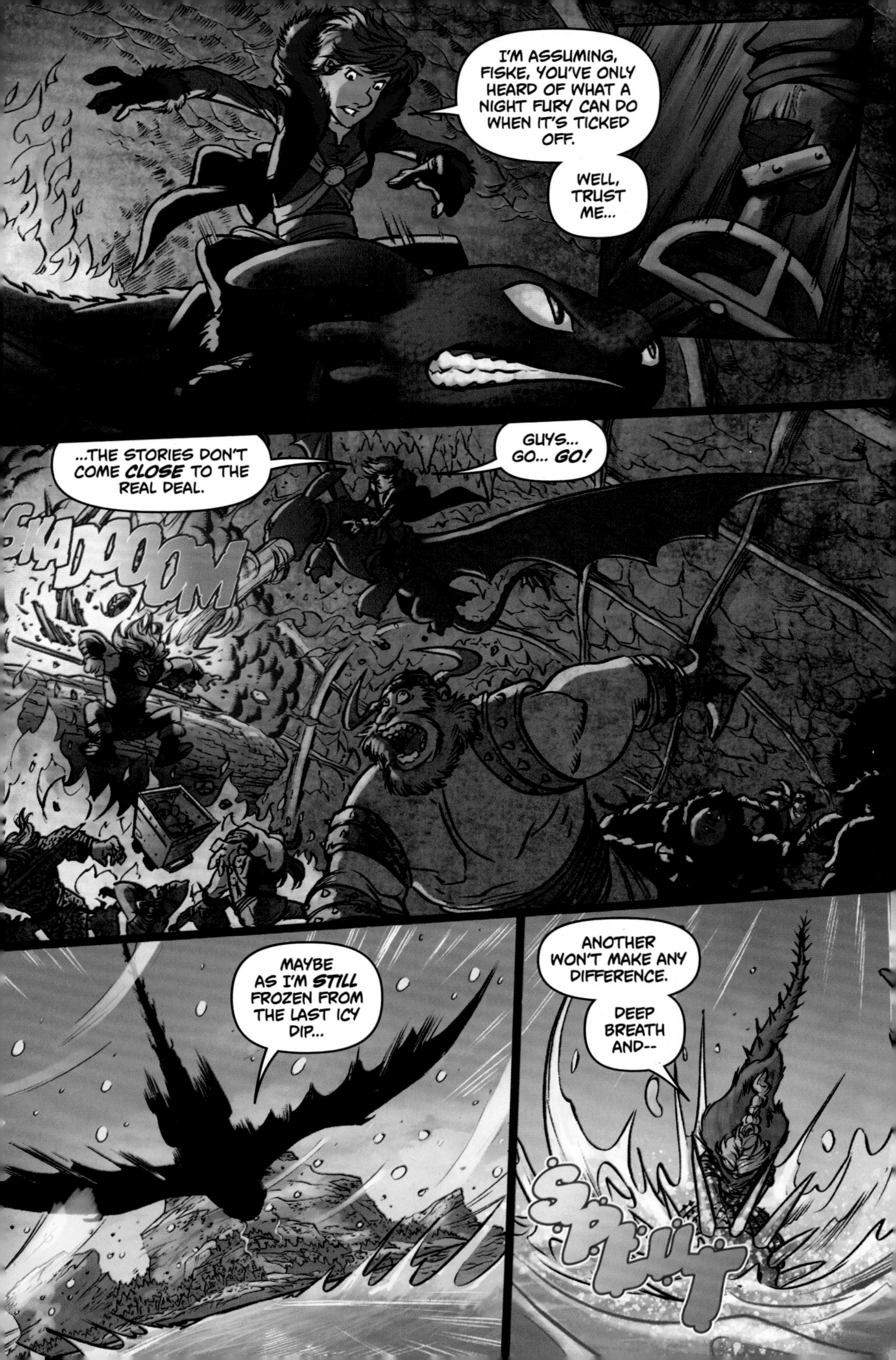
I'M ASSUMING, FISKE, YOU'VE ONLY HEARD OF WHAT A NIGHT FURY CAN DO WHEN IT'S TICKED OFF.
WELL, TRUST ME...
...THE STORIES DON'T COME CLOSE TO THE REAL DEAL.
GUYS... GO... GO!
SKADOOOM
MAYBE AS I'M STILL FROZEN FROM THE LAST ICY DIP...
ANOTHER WON'T MAKE ANY DIFFERENCE.
DEEP BREATH AND--
SPLUT

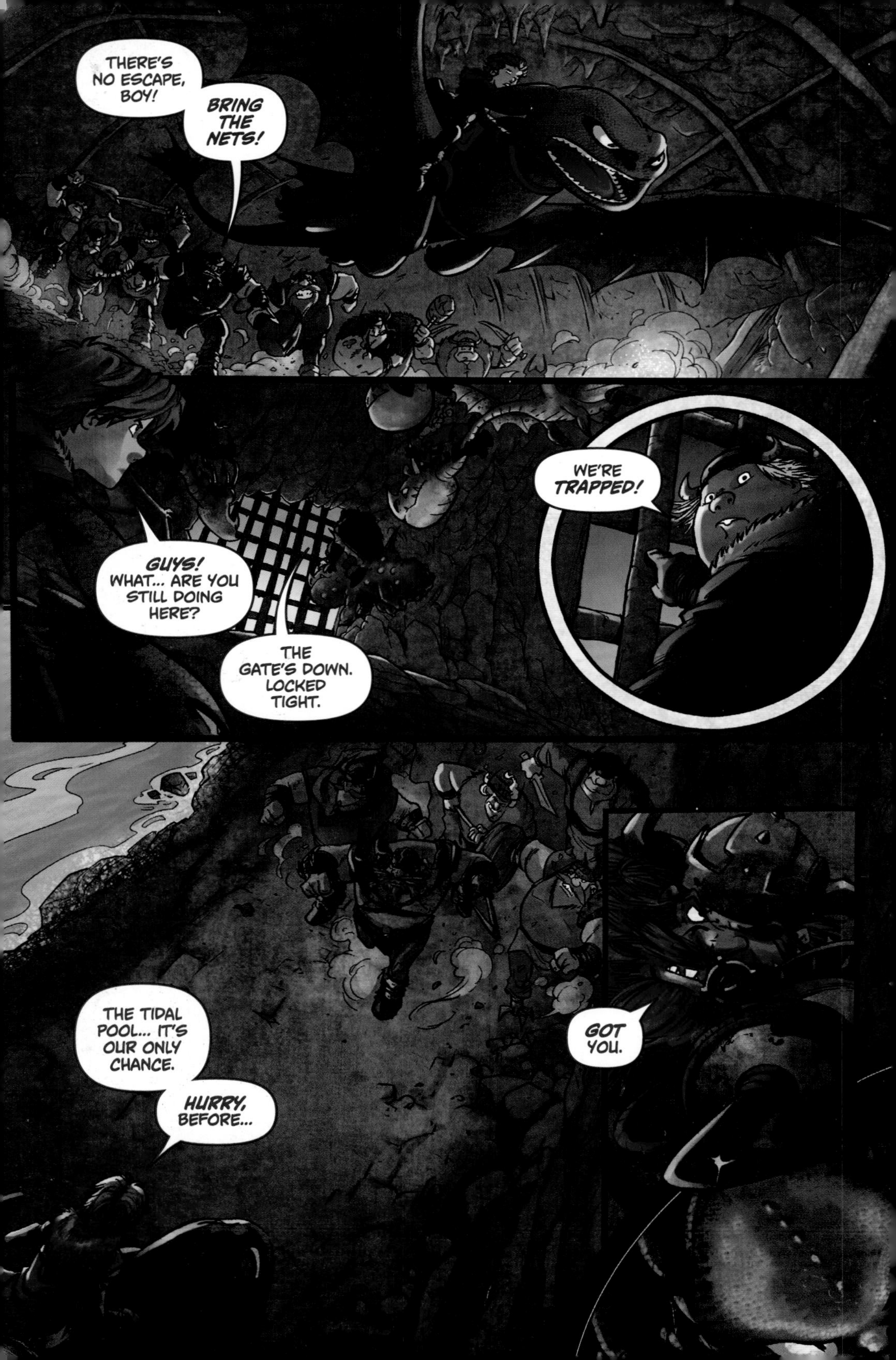
THERE'S NO ESCAPE, BOY!
BRING THE NETS!
GUYS! WHAT... ARE YOU STILL DOING HERE?
THE GATE'S DOWN. LOCKED TIGHT.
WE'RE TRAPPED!
THE TIDAL POOL... IT'S OUR ONLY CHANCE.
HURRY, BEFORE...
GOT YOU.

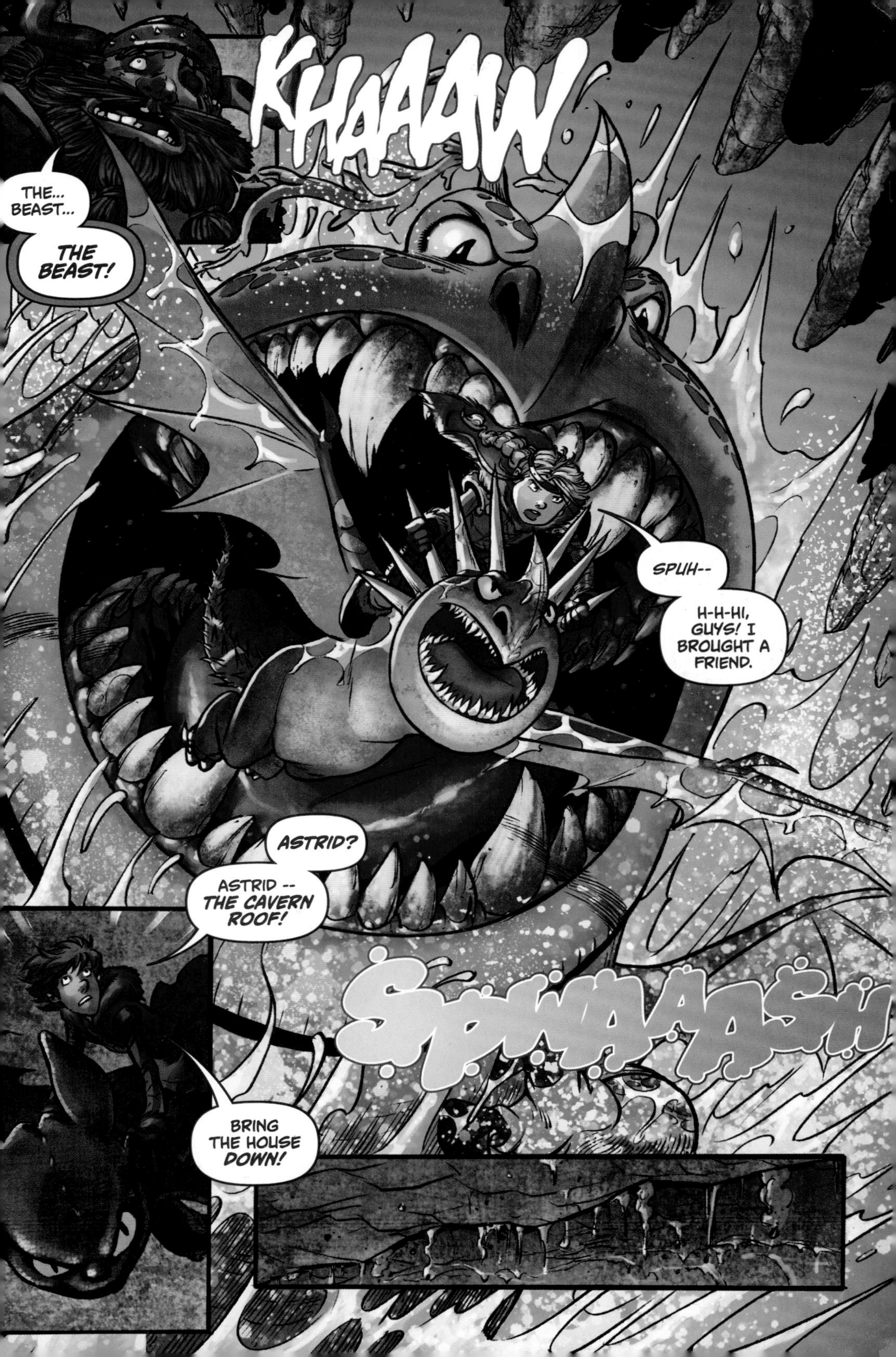
KHAAAW
THE... BEAST...
THE BEAST!
SPUH--
H-H-HI, GUYS! I BROUGHT A FRIEND.
ASTRID?
ASTRID -- THE CAVERN ROOF!
SPWAAASH
BRING THE HOUSE DOWN!

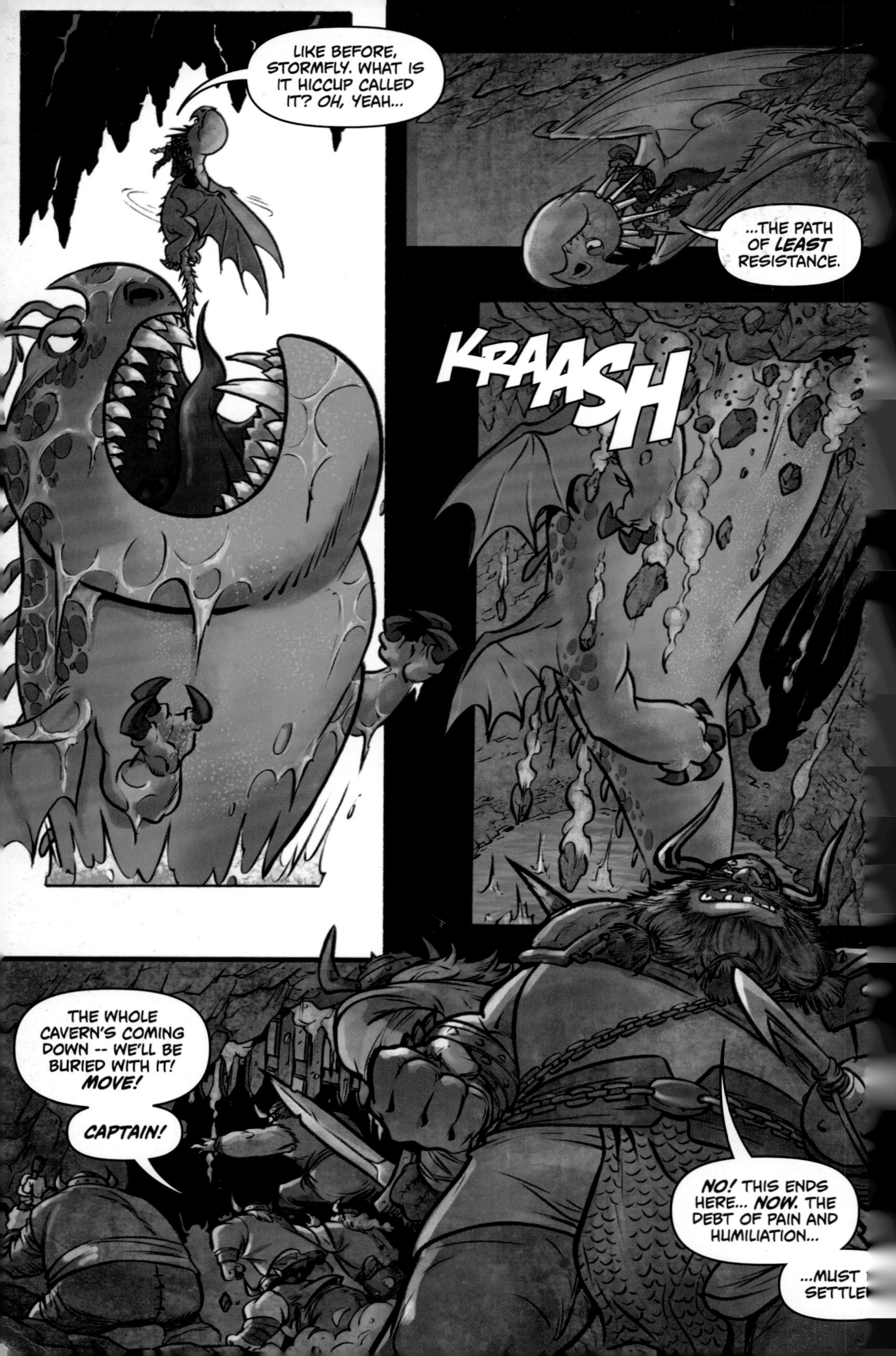
LIKE BEFORE, STORMFLY. WHAT IS IT HICCUP CALLED IT? OH, YEAH...
...THE PATH OF LEAST RESISTANCE.
KRAASH
THE WHOLE CAVERN'S COMING DOWN -- WE'LL BE BURIED WITH IT! MOVE!
CAPTAIN!
NO! THIS ENDS HERE... NOW. THE DEBT OF PAIN AND HUMILIATION...
...MUST

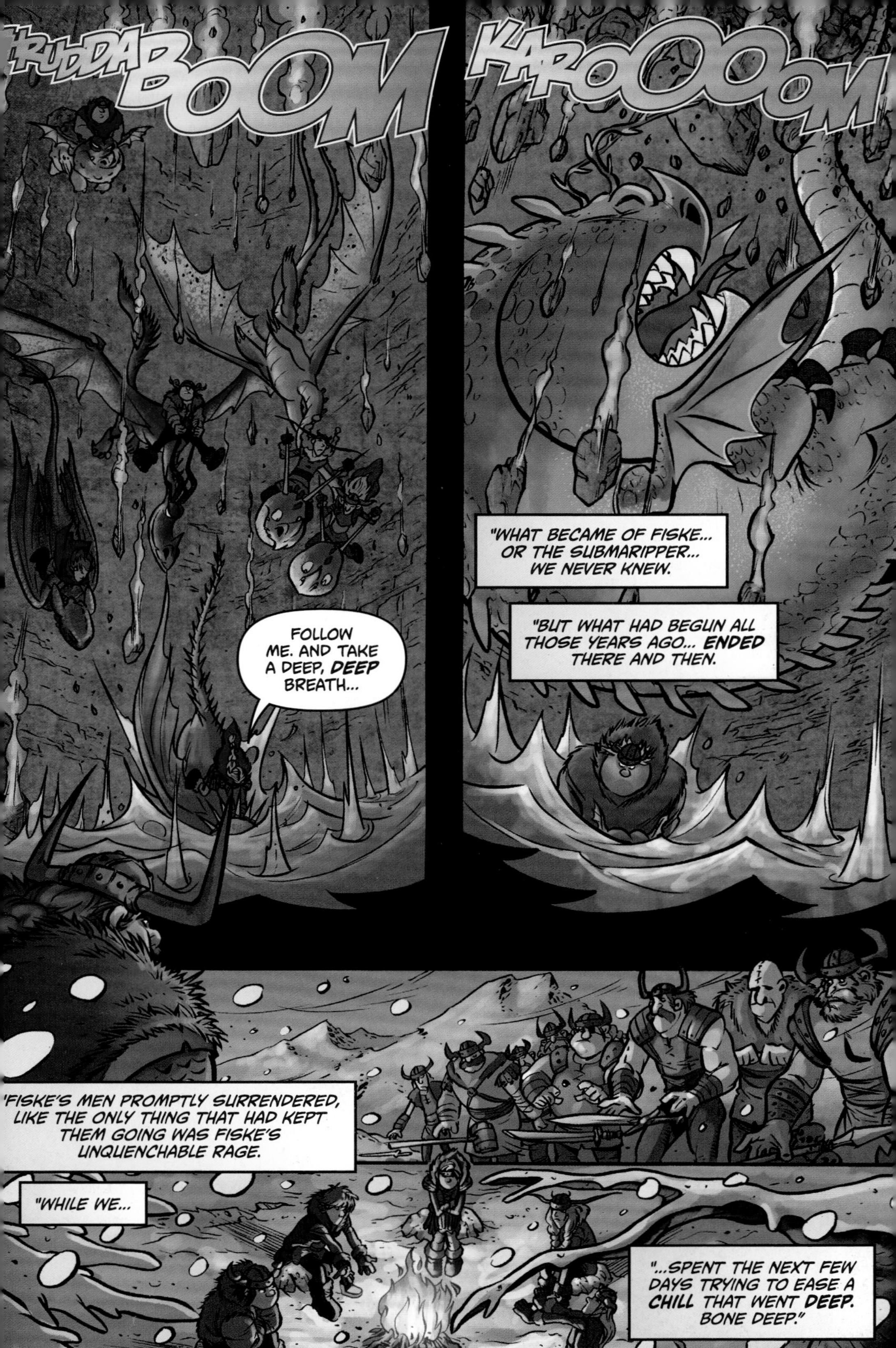
THRUDDA BOOOM
FOLLOW ME. AND TAKE A DEEP, DEEP BREATH...
KAROOOOOM
"WHAT BECAME OF FISKE... OR THE SUBMARIPPER... WE NEVER KNEW.
"BUT WHAT HAD BEGUN ALL THOSE YEARS AGO... ENDED THERE AND THEN.
"FISKE'S MEN PROMPTLY SURRENDERED, LIKE THE ONLY THING THAT HAD KEPT THEM GOING WAS FISKE'S UNQUENCHABLE RAGE.
"WHILE WE...
"...SPENT THE NEXT FEW DAYS TRYING TO EASE A CHILL THAT WENT DEEP. BONE DEEP."

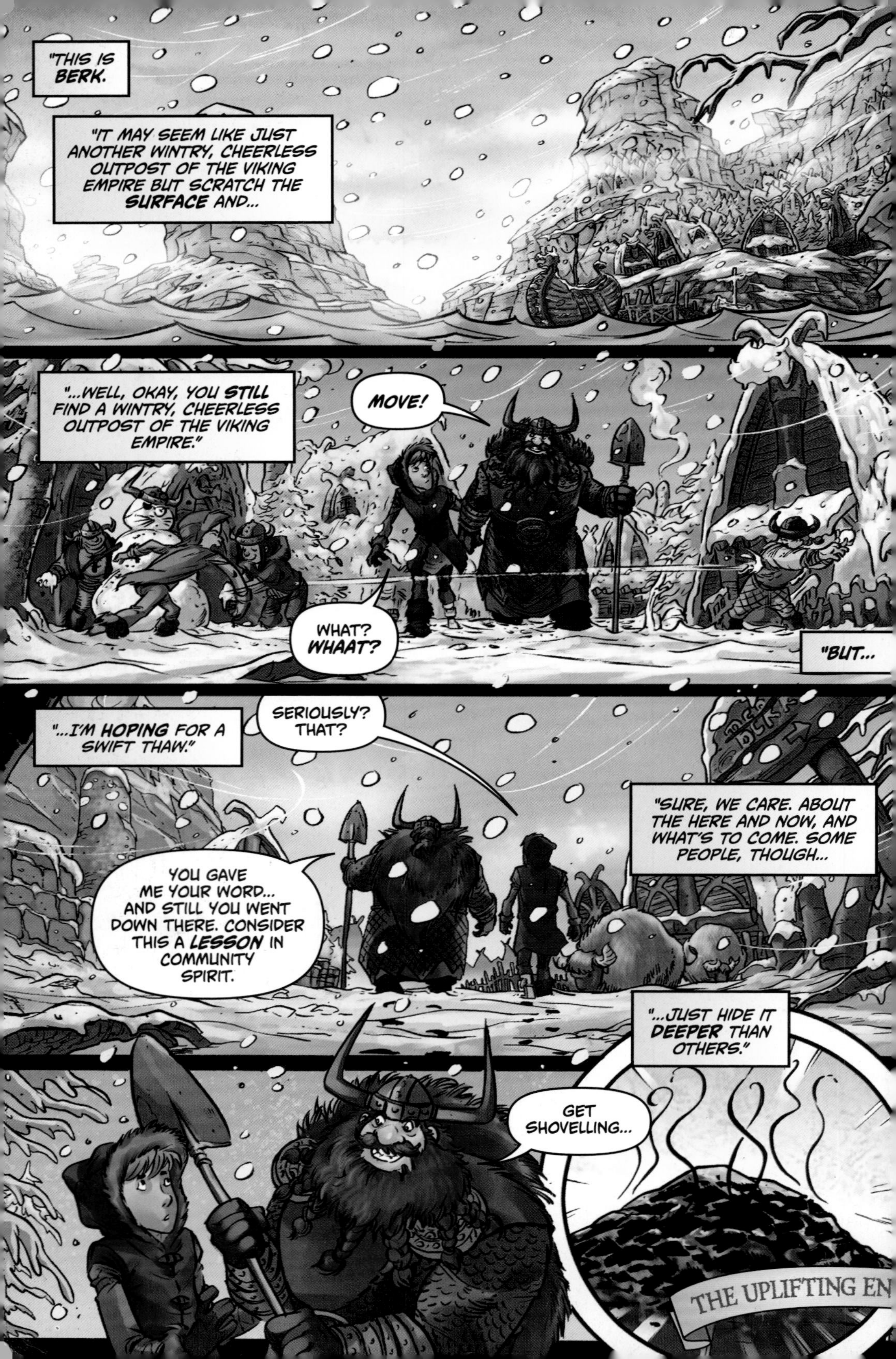
"THIS IS BERK.
"IT MAY SEEM LIKE JUST ANOTHER WINTRY, CHEERLESS OUTPOST OF THE VIKING EMPIRE BUT SCRATCH THE SURFACE AND...
"...WELL, OKAY, YOU STILL FIND A WINTRY, CHEERLESS OUTPOST OF THE VIKING EMPIRE."
MOVE!
WHAT? WHAAT?
"BUT...
"...I'M HOPING FOR A SWIFT THAW."
SERIOUSLY? THAT?
YOU GAVE ME YOUR WORD... AND STILL YOU WENT DOWN THERE. CONSIDER THIS A LESSON IN COMMUNITY SPIRIT.
"SURE, WE CARE. ABOUT THE HERE AND NOW, AND WHAT'S TO COME. SOME PEOPLE, THOUGH...
"...JUST HIDE IT DEEPER THAN OTHERS."
GET SHOVELLING...
THE UPLIFTING EN

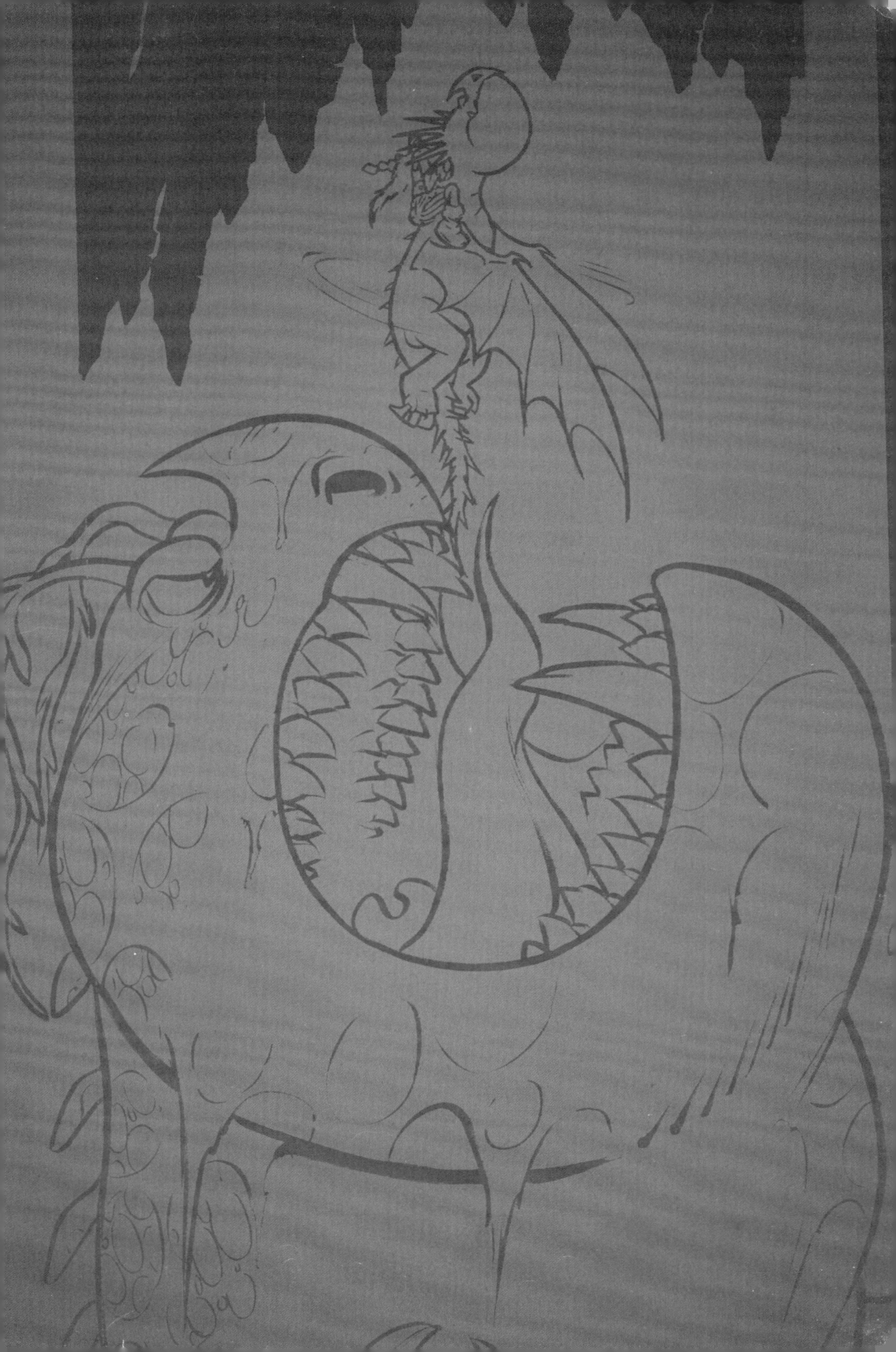

SMELTDOWN

WRITER
SIMON FURMAN

ARTIST
ARIANNA FLOREAN

COLORS
CLAUDIA IANICIELLO

LETTERS
JIM CAMPBELL

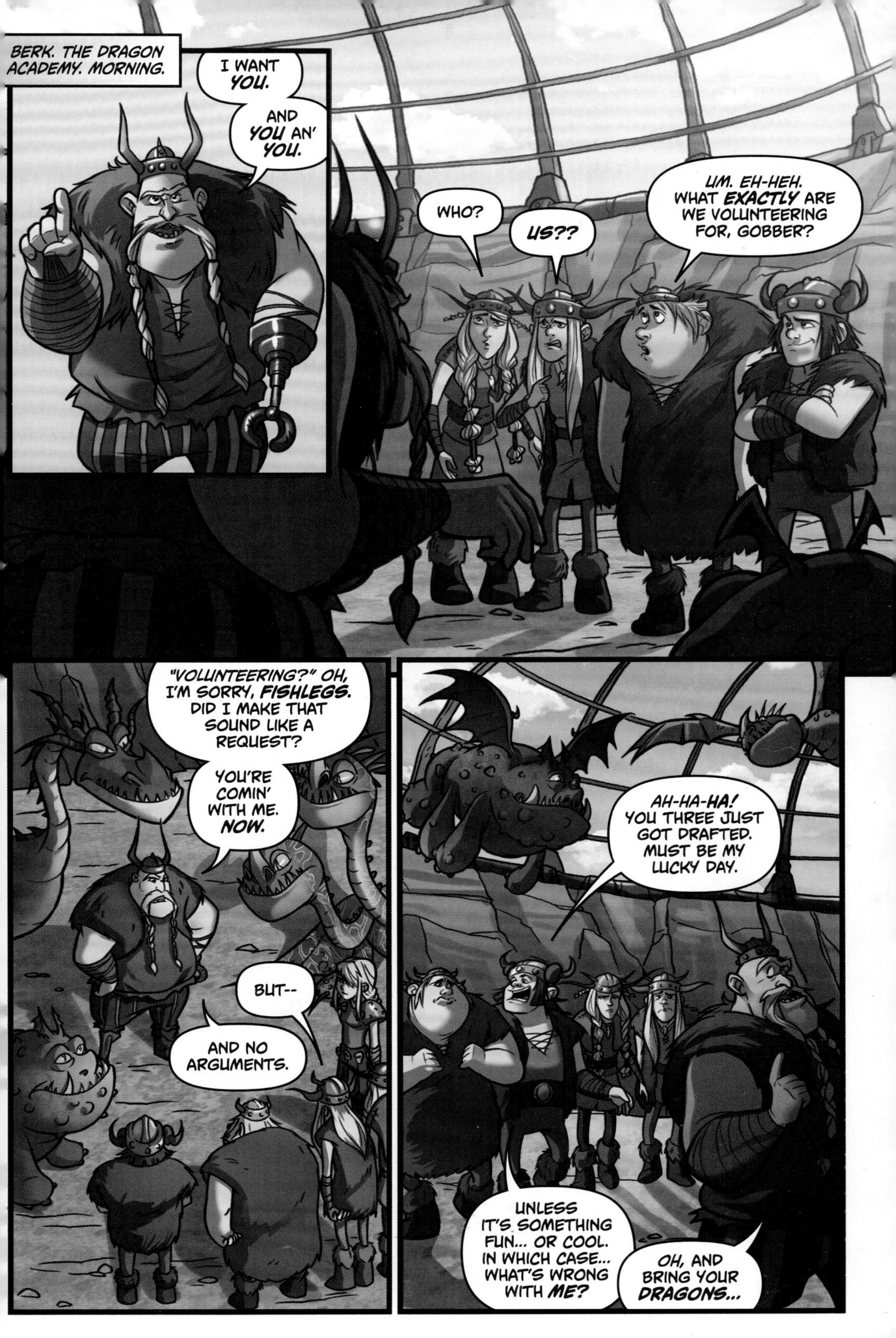
BERK. THE DRAGON ACADEMY. MORNING.
I WANT YOU.
AND YOU AN' YOU.
WHO?
US??
UM. EH-HEH. WHAT EXACTLY ARE WE VOLUNTEERING FOR, GOBBER?
"VOLUNTEERING?" OH, I'M SORRY, FISHLEGS. DID I MAKE THAT SOUND LIKE A REQUEST?
YOU'RE COMIN' WITH ME. NOW.
BUT--
AND NO ARGUMENTS.
AH-HA-HA! YOU THREE JUST GOT DRAFTED. MUST BE MY LUCKY DAY.
UNLESS IT'S SOMETHING FUN... OR COOL. IN WHICH CASE... WHAT'S WRONG WITH ME?
OH, AND BRING YOUR DRAGONS...

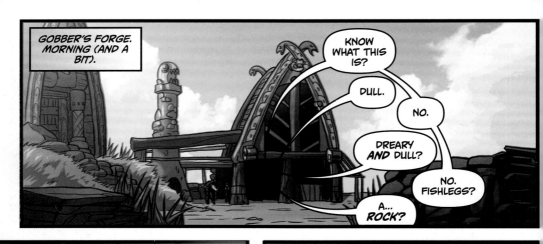

GOBBER'S FORGE. MORNING (AND A BIT).

KNOW WHAT THIS IS?

DULL.

NO.

DREARY *AND* DULL?

NO. FISHLEGS?

A... *ROCK?*

AN *ORE-BEARING* ROCK. NOW *HICCUP* HERE HAS BEEN TELLING ME ALL ABOUT CAPTAIN FISKE'S UNDERGROUND MINING OPERATION, AND IT GOT ME THINKING...

WELL, OKAY, IT GOT *HICCUP* THINKING. I JUST NODDED MY HEAD NOW AND THEN.

HICCUP...

SO IT OCCURRED TO ME THAT WE COULD PRODUCE DOUBLE THE METAL, TWICE AS QUICKLY...

...IF WE USED *DRAGON* POWER IN THE SMELTING PROCESS.

I GIVE YOU... THE FLAME-TASTIC INFERNO-CLASS *FIREPOWER-PLUS!*

I GIVE IT... HALF A DAY. THEN -- CALAMITY AND RUIN.

I'LL RAISE YOU CARNAGE AND CATASTROPHE BY MID-MORNING... TOP LOSER TIDIES THE DRAGON PENS.

YOU'RE ON.

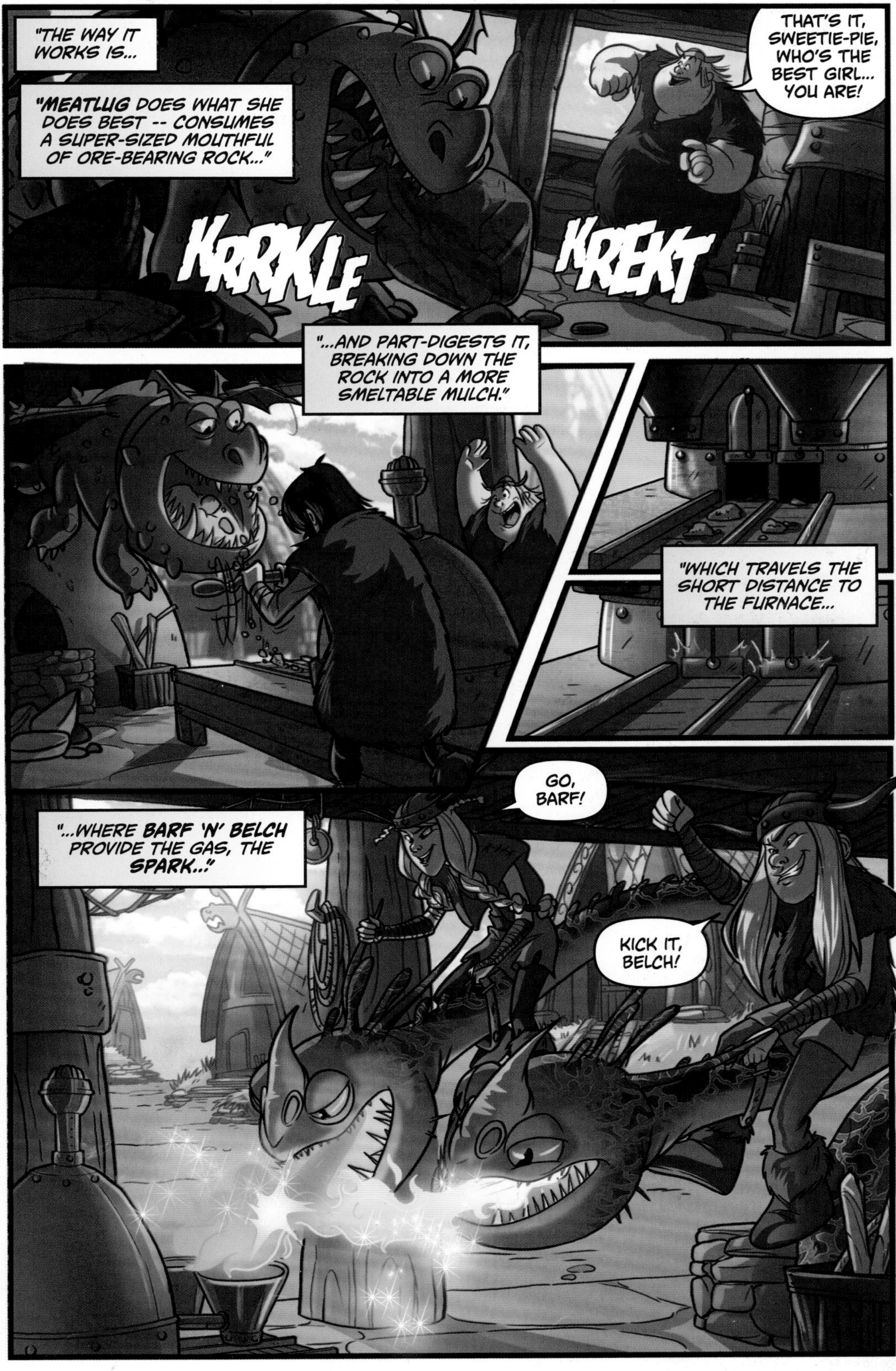
"THE WAY IT WORKS IS...
"MEATLUG DOES WHAT SHE DOES BEST -- CONSUMES A SUPER-SIZED MOUTHFUL OF ORE-BEARING ROCK..."
THAT'S IT, SWEETIE-PIE, WHO'S THE BEST GIRL... YOU ARE!
KRRKLE
KREKT
"...AND PART-DIGESTS IT, BREAKING DOWN THE ROCK INTO A MORE SMELTABLE MULCH."
"WHICH TRAVELS THE SHORT DISTANCE TO THE FURNACE...
"...WHERE BARF 'N' BELCH PROVIDE THE GAS, THE SPARK..."
GO, BARF!
KICK IT, BELCH!

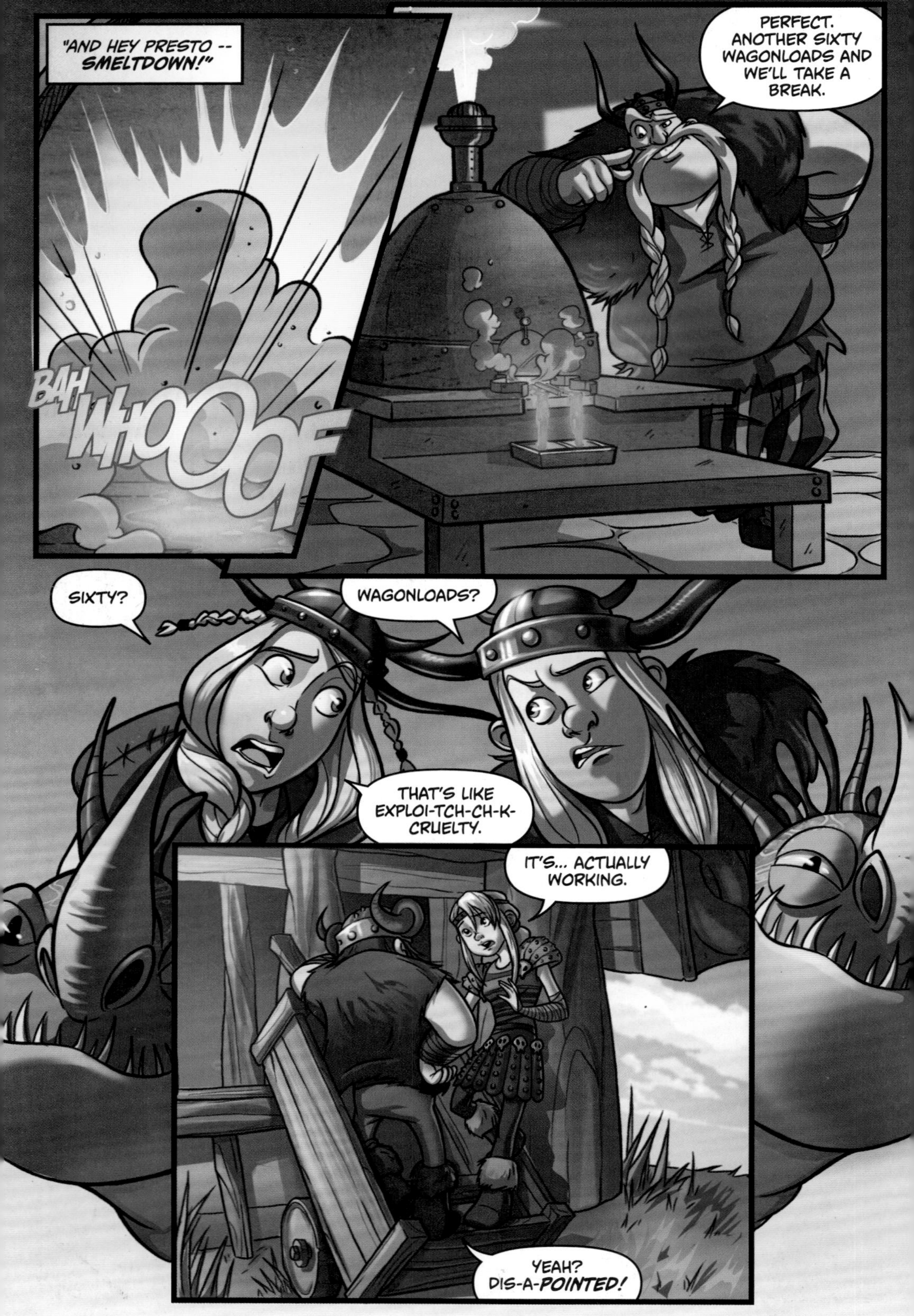
"AND HEY PRESTO -- SMELTDOWN!"
BAH WHOOOOF
PERFECT. ANOTHER SIXTY WAGONLOADS AND WE'LL TAKE A BREAK.
SIXTY?
WAGONLOADS?
THAT'S LIKE EXPLOI-TCH-CH-K-CRUELTY.
IT'S... ACTUALLY WORKING.
YEAH? DIS-A-POINTED!

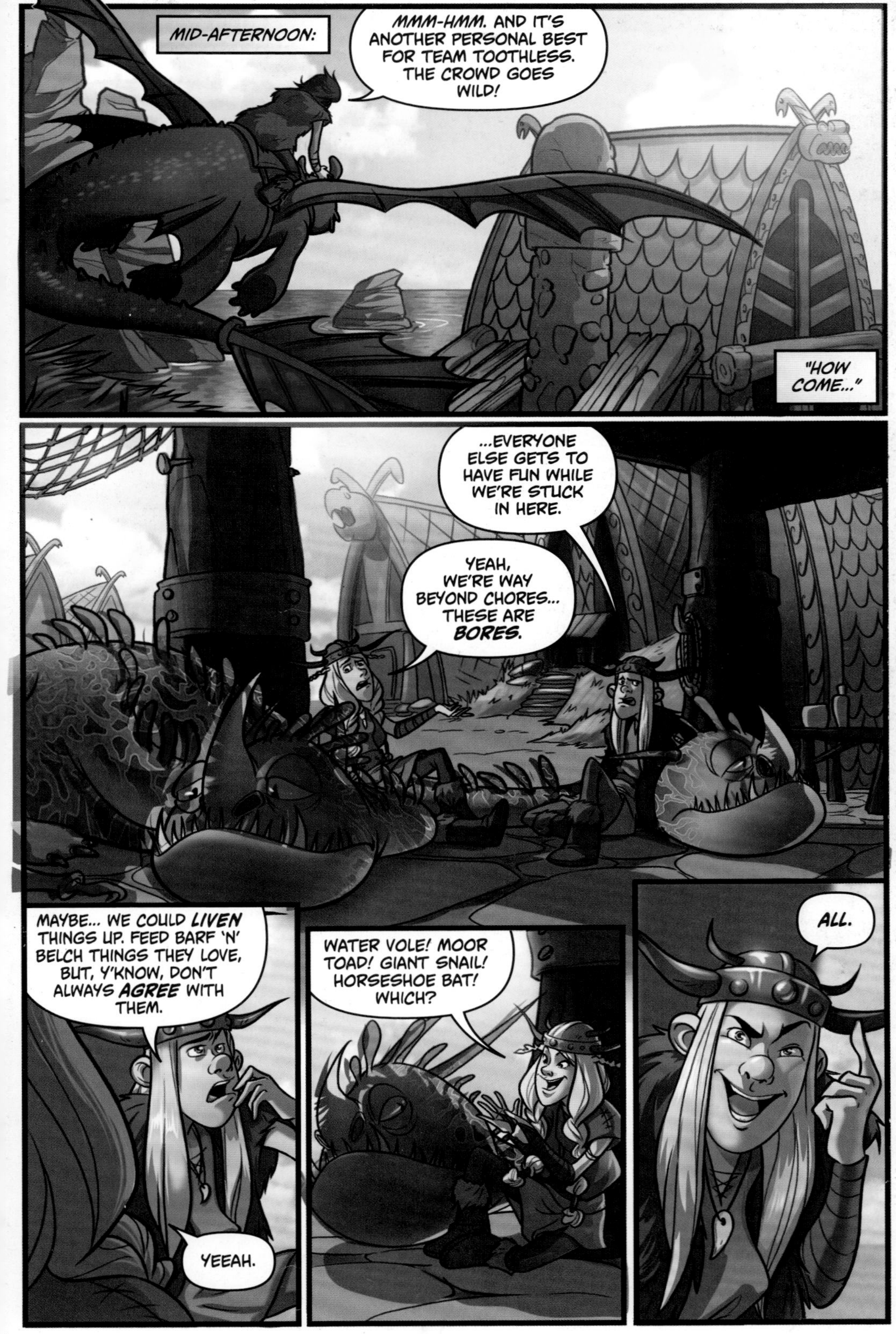
MID-AFTERNOON:
MMM-HMM. AND IT'S ANOTHER PERSONAL BEST FOR TEAM TOOTHLESS. THE CROWD GOES WILD!
"HOW COME..."
...EVERYONE ELSE GETS TO HAVE FUN WHILE WE'RE STUCK IN HERE.
YEAH, WE'RE WAY BEYOND CHORES... THESE ARE BORES.
MAYBE... WE COULD LIVEN THINGS UP. FEED BARF 'N' BELCH THINGS THEY LOVE, BUT, Y'KNOW, DON'T ALWAYS AGREE WITH THEM.
YEEAH.
WATER VOLE! MOOR TOAD! GIANT SNAIL! HORSESHOE BAT! WHICH?
ALL.

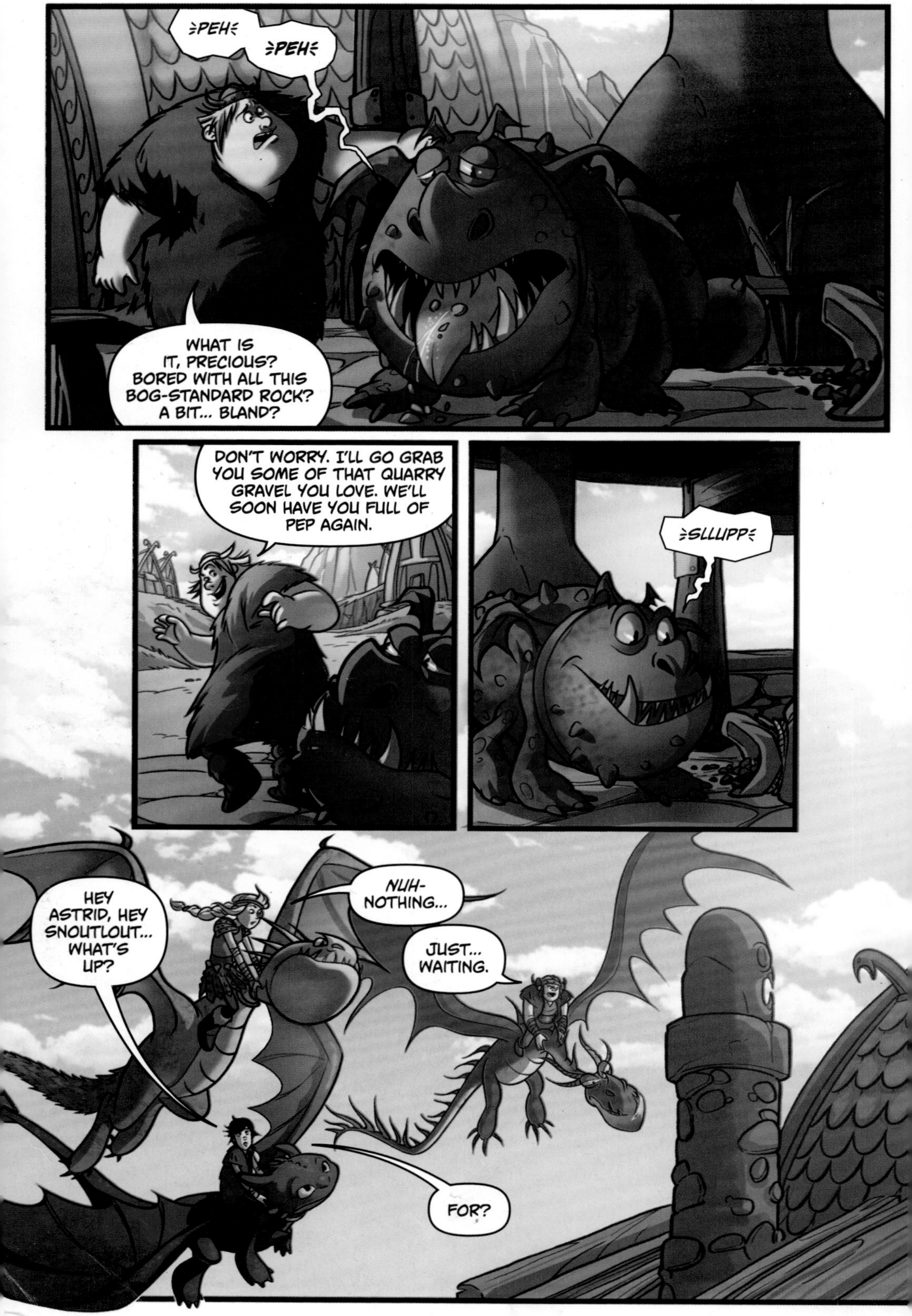

PEH
PEH
WHAT IS IT, PRECIOUS? BORED WITH ALL THIS BOG-STANDARD ROCK? A BIT... BLAND?
DON'T WORRY. I'LL GO GRAB YOU SOME OF THAT QUARRY GRAVEL YOU LOVE. WE'LL SOON HAVE YOU FULL OF PEP AGAIN.
SLLUPP
HEY ASTRID, HEY SNOUTLOUT... WHAT'S UP?
NUH-NOTHING...
JUST... WAITING.
FOR?

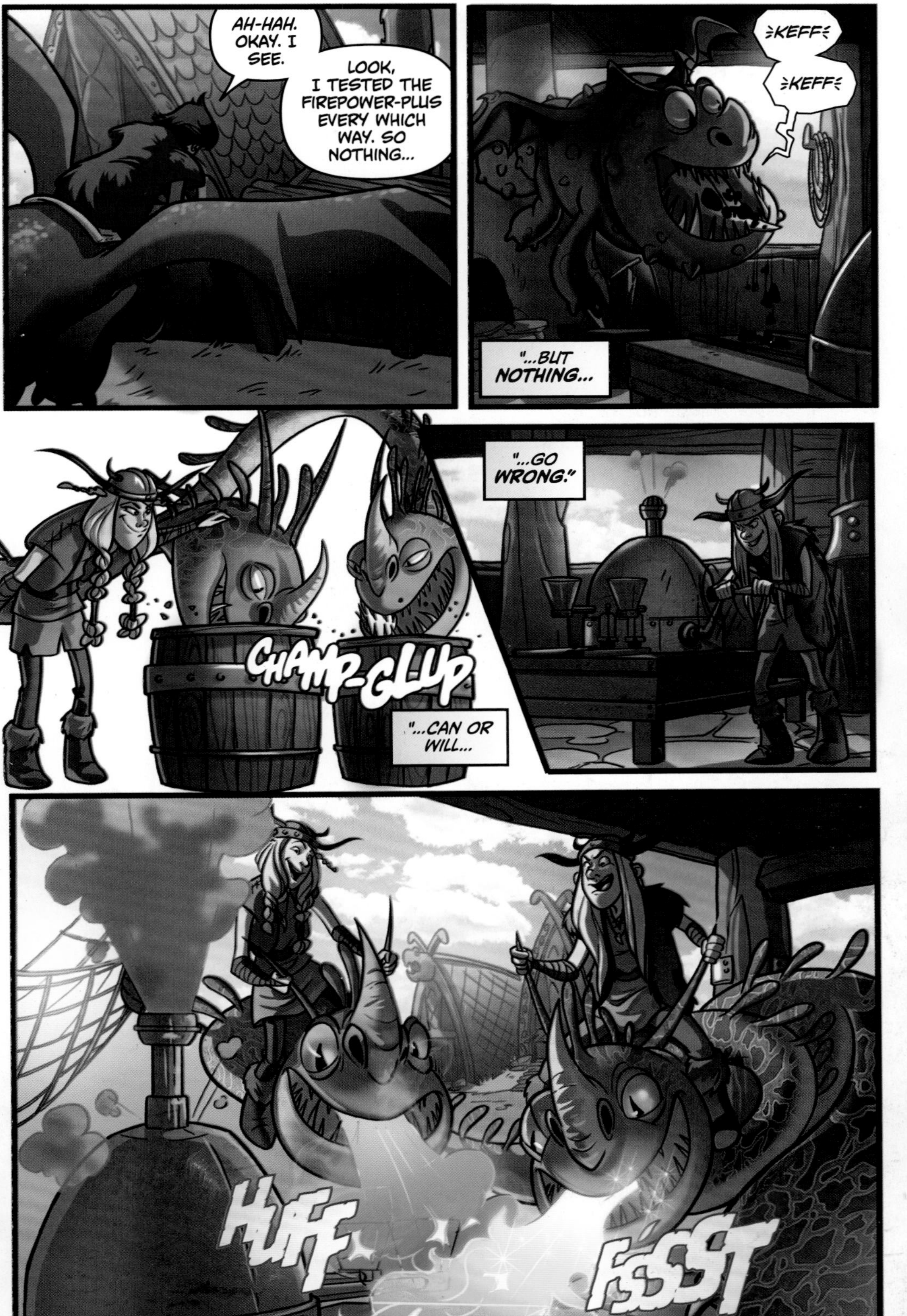
AH-HAH. OKAY. I SEE.
LOOK, I TESTED THE FIREPOWER-PLUS EVERY WHICH WAY. SO NOTHING...
KEFF
KEFF
"...BUT NOTHING...
CHAMP-GLUP
"...CAN OR WILL...
"...GO WRONG."
HUFF
FSSST

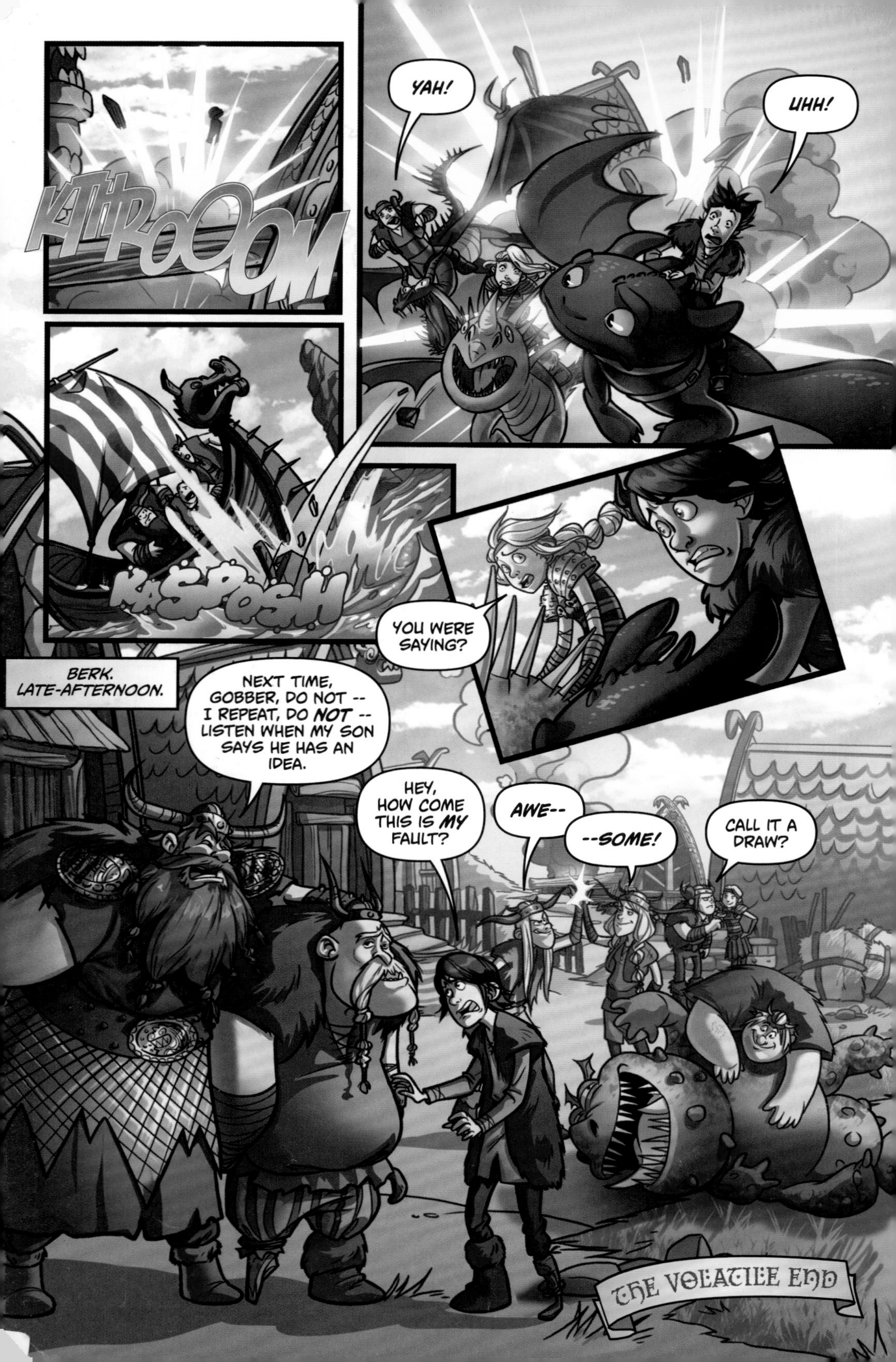
KTHROOOM
YAH!
UHH!
KASPOSH
YOU WERE SAYING?
BERK. LATE-AFTERNOON.
NEXT TIME, GOBBER, DO NOT -- I REPEAT, DO NOT -- LISTEN WHEN MY SON SAYS HE HAS AN IDEA.
HEY, HOW COME THIS IS MY FAULT?
AWE--
--SOME!
CALL IT A DRAW?
THE VOLATILE END

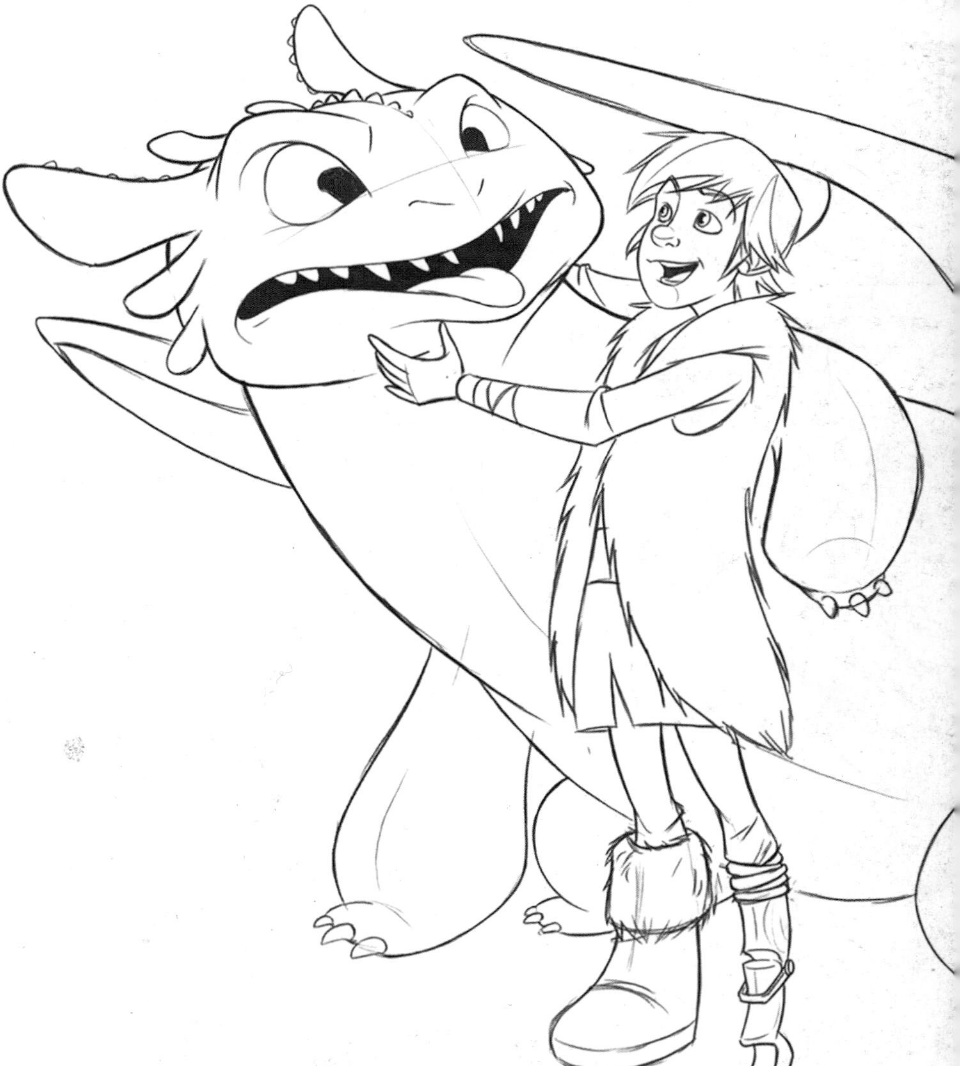

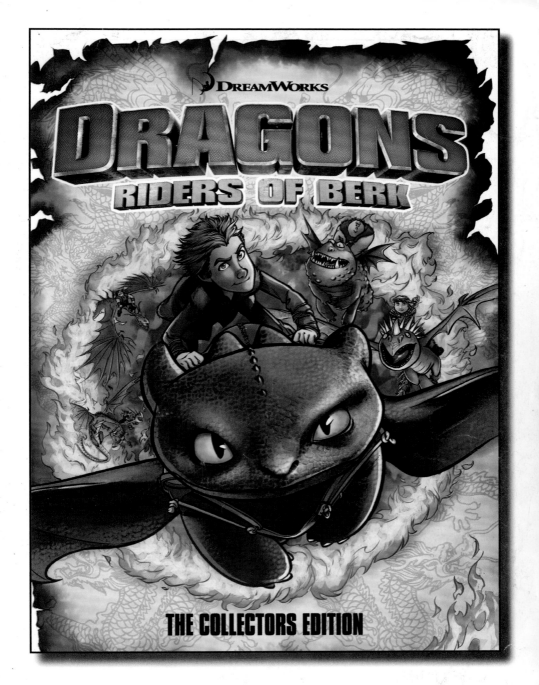

DREAMWORKS DRAGONS: RIDERS OF BERK
– THE COLLECTORS EDITION

This beautiful hardback book collects the first two volumes of
Titan Publishing's critically acclaimed *DreamWorks Dragons: Riders
of Berk* series. Plus, some amazing 'behind the scenes' extras!
On sale November 2015!

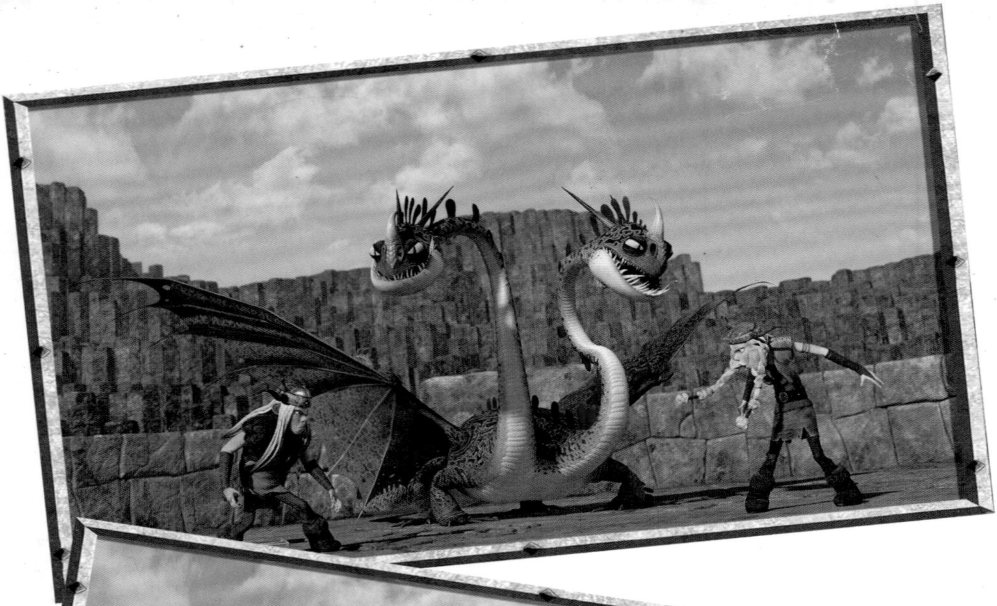

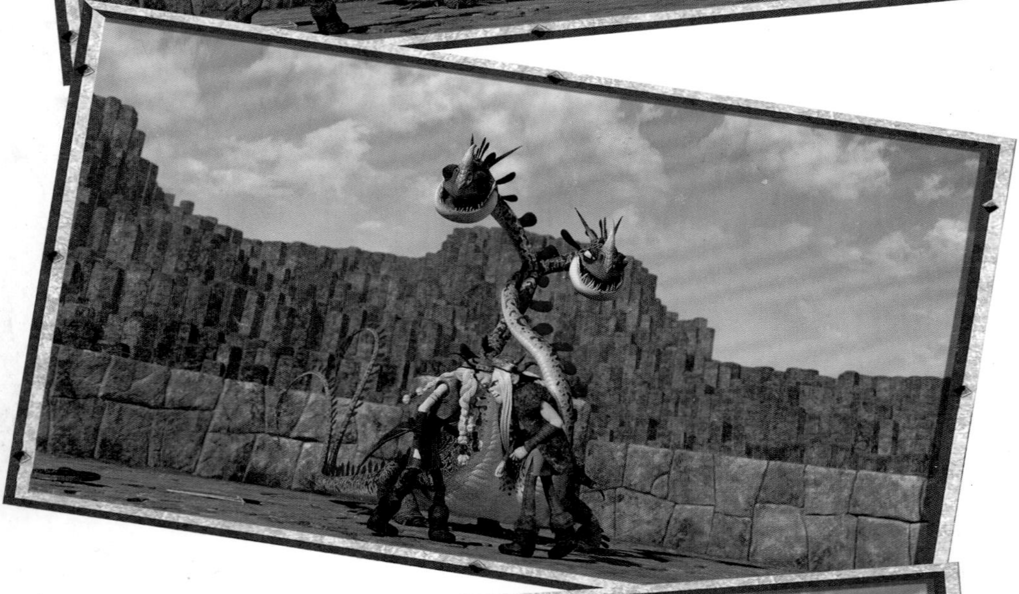

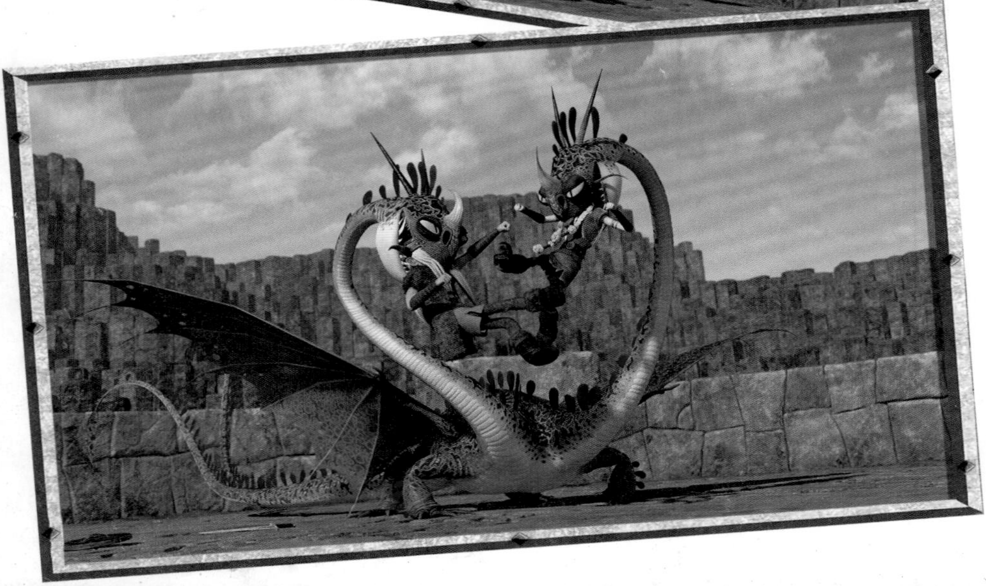